Lexile 780

Points 7

Unfinished Portrait of Jessica

ALSO BY RICHARD PECK

NOVELS FOR YOUNG PEOPLE

Don't Look and It Won't Hurt

Dreamland Lake

Through a Brief Darkness

Representing Super Doll

The Ghost Belonged to Me

Ghosts I Have Been

Are You in the House Alone?

Father Figure

Secrets of the Shopping Mall

Close Enough to Touch

The Dreadful Future of Blossom Culp

Remembering the Good Times

Blossom Culp and the Sleep of Death

Princess Ashley

Those Summer Girls I Never Met

Voices After Midnight

NOVELS FOR ADULTS

Amanda/Miranda

New York Time

This Family of Women

PICTURE BOOKS

Monster Night at Grandma's House
(Illustrated by Don Freeman)

NONFICTION ANTHOLOGIES

Edge of Awareness (Coedited with Ned E. Hoopes)

Leap into Reality

VERSE ANTHOLOGIES

Sounds and Silences

Mindscapes

Pictures That Storm Inside My Head

17564

Unfinished Portrait of Jessica

by Richard Peck

Delacorte Press

Published by
Delacorte Press
Bantam Doubleday Dell Publishing Group, Inc.
666 Fifth Avenue
New York, New York 10103

Library of Congress Cataloging in Publication Data
Peck, Richard, [date of birth]
    Unfinished portrait of Jessica / by Richard Peck
        p. cm.
    Summary: A trip to Mexico to visit the divorced vagabond father whom she
idolizes cures fourteen-year-old Jessica of certain illusions and helps her
reconstruct her relationship with her mother.
    ISBN 0-385-30500-1
    [1. Fathers and daughters—Fiction. 2. Mothers and daughters—Fiction.
3. Mexico—Fiction. 4. Divorce—Fiction.] I. Title.
PZ7.P338Un 1991
[Fic]—dc20   91-6780
                                                                   CIP
                                                                    AC

Designed by Paul Zakris

Manufactured in the United States of America

November 1991

10 9 8 7 6 5 4 3 2

BVG

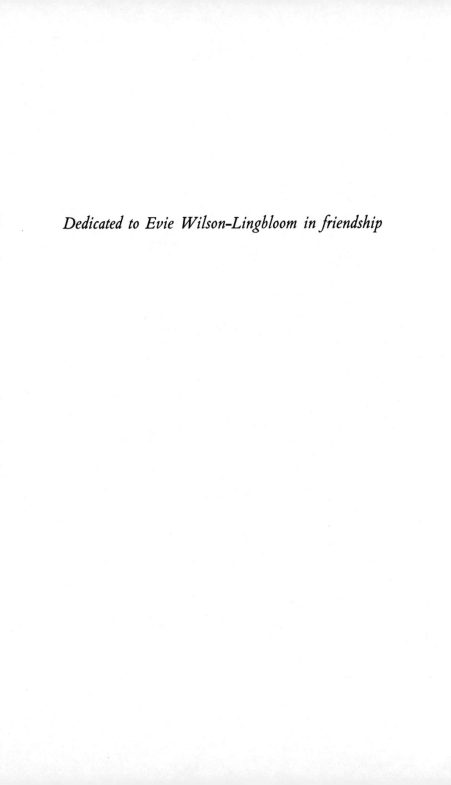

Dedicated to Evie Wilson-Lingbloom in friendship

AMOR

Burned into my memory is a house rising among rocks above a bay. It stands in another world from mine, like a dream in primary colors, and yet it refuses to let me leave. Every hot day of summer recalls winter there. The sea wavers in heat. The sun throws combs of light through the palm leaves.

It's a house in a land where something is always dying in plain sight, and yet nature heals. It creates sand from ashes, and soil from sand, and then flowers to screen and promise. There's salt in the sand there, salt from the sea, and so the terraces crumble at their edges. Even the earth is liable to open at your feet just when you were sure of your ground.

The house has a very Mexican name, **Amor y Muerte** *—Love and Death. But I knew nothing of love and death the first time I went there. I was fourteen.*

CHAPTER 1

NOT EVEN FOURTEEN YET. I WAS STILL DAYS AWAY
from fourteen, and they were plodding, icebound
days. A hard frost patterned every pane of the window. In the December blackness outside, ice groaned
on the lake. Farther south, where Lake Shore Drive
curves, Michigan Avenue had begun to glitter with
the white pinpoint lights of Christmas.

When I was little, I was a princess in this tower.
The turrets stood brave above the lake, and the ivy
rattled on the high walls until winter scoured the
leaves away. Now it was the apartment building it had
always been. Most of what I used to think didn't work
anymore.

I was in my room now every night. I needed to be

there, in a safe shell of Walkman-sound blaring whatever tape proved you were a teenager that year. But I didn't dare. I needed to keep my ears free to hear every sound.

It was the room I'd always had, with the old crystal doorknobs and the indefinite-blue walls. My bulletin board was above the desk, and a foggy mirror hung on the closet door. I'd angled it to reflect me, and I'd propped a big pad of bond paper on my knees. I was trying a charcoal sketch of myself, the self-portrait of Jessica Ferris. An artistic strain threaded through the family, my father's family, and I wondered if it had found me.

But I couldn't seem to find myself, not on the white, oversized paper. I was working a little larger than life, which magnified everything wrong with the picture, or with my face. The eyes were wrong. I had no idea how to make charcoal represent blue. The nose was nowhere, and my hair was someone else's, because I'd never liked mine. I'd only captured my neck, a too stringy stem. Lower than that I wouldn't go.

I didn't have a clue about working in charcoal. I only liked the faint sound the black, crumbly stick made on the toothed paper. And I was listening, holding my breath to hear. I thought my mother must be just outside the door.

The apartment was so quiet that I heard distant sounds from other floors. A radiator clumped somewhere, and a heel scraped. Something that wasn't quite a sound whispered in the sway of the curtains. But if my mother was just beyond the door, she'd be silent, her feet in soft slippers, her cheek against the varnished wood; listening, hearing my thoughts.

My homework was on the desk, and I half hoped she'd come in to see I wasn't doing it. Beside me on the bed was a book, not a schoolbook. It was a novel by Angela Chatsworth that I'd been reading, devouring. *Love's Incandescence.*

It was about a young woman, not so many years older than I was, but beautiful. She was there on the cover, her perfect profile turned up to her dark lover. His square hand gripped her arm. Behind them, at the end of a long double row of trees, a tall English castle stood. No, Scottish. Her lover was English, but she was a Scotswoman, and that difference symbolized all the differences between them. She belonged to a clan and wore a long sweep of tartan over her full white dress. Whenever I read, I felt the skirts caressing her legs. Some passages I had by heart.

There were wicked people in the story, keeping the lovers apart, people who spied and lied. But on page 140 she'd been liberated by her lover's sealing kiss. I felt the kiss warm on my lips and hoped it would last.

But there were dark corners in her lover's mind, and three hundred pages still to go. I'd looked up the word "incandescence." It meant "emission of visible light by a hot object."

Then, like a nightmare something winked in the room, and I saw the doorknob turn. The charcoal in my hand slashed across the drawing pad, throwing black sparks. But I was ready for her. I stuffed the pad down the far side of the bed, because she wasn't to see my drawing. It was of me and too personal, and not very good. I reached for _Love's Incandescence_ with blackened hands.

I was ready for her because I'd known all along she was outside. She might have been there all evening, taking silent breaths. Over these last months I'd been waking up in the night, wondering how near she was.

She may just have brushed the door with her knuckles, pretending to knock. Now she was on the threshold, as if I'd ask her to come in. From the corner of my eye I saw her notice the book in my hands. I supposed she thought it was a trashy novel. It wasn't. It was wonderful, but I hoped she'd think it was trashy. Her glasses had worked down her nose, and she was wearing the bathrobe she said she did her thinking in. I hoped not to hear her thoughts.

"Hot chocolate?" she said. "In the microwave."

I pored over the book and put a finger with a ragged nail on a random word. When she was gone, I looked up to see that she'd left the door open, to make me get up and close it.

At the door I jerked another knot in the sash of my robe and decided to go on to the kitchen for her hot chocolate, to keep her from coming back with it. But I turned back to my room, tempting myself to stay. I still thought there might be safe places.

I'd already put away most of the things from childhood, the stuffed things and the Beverly Clearys. There wasn't much in the room now, in case she came in to go through my drawers when I was gone during the day. I'd have carried all my letters to school with me, if I had any letters. Lately I'd been pretending it was a hotel room and I'd be checking out tomorrow.

But I'd kept my bulletin board and turned it into a kind of collage featuring my father. Pictures of him at all ages, and pictures he'd taken. He was a photographer—Scott Ferris—a brilliant one, I thought. He was the sort who'd shoot a dozen rolls of film for one perfect shot of an old barn etched in sunlight. Or a field of wheat moving like the sea. I had his photographs pinned up, mainly his rejects. But most of the pictures were of him at all ages. A big one in washed-out color when he was a little boy, bare-kneed on a bench, with a smile shy and sly. And his senior-year picture with funny sideburns and his face not quite squared off yet. A picture of a keg party in college, a group picture, but he stands out in it. The light catches him and leaves the others in shadow. The pictures overlapped the bulletin board and had begun to crawl across the wall.

Forty of his faces at least, among his shots of dew-drenched spider webs and one or two of me taken a long time ago. Once, maybe only once, we'd gone to the playground off Astor Street. He shot a roll of film of me in my snowsuit on a swing. A winter day, and so it was only the two of us there, at first. I was airborne in the swing, feeling the sting of the cold on my face. My father, this grown-up playmate, had crouched in front of me, recording the moment. It hung now by pins on the bulletin board, caught like a butterfly.

There'd been another moment in the playground that afternoon. Suddenly, like a meeting, a lady was there with us, sitting in another swing. At first I thought it was my mother because every lady seemed to be my mother then. She was a stranger though, to me, and I thought it was funny that she'd be sitting in a child's swing. She knew my dad. They talked and laughed behind me, uncautious because I was a little older than they knew. He swung me higher, up to the top floors of buildings, beyond roofs until all I saw was white sky. When I came down, he wasn't by my swing. He was beside hers, and her hand was on his sleeve, and he was whispering to her; a secret, I suppose. We stayed at the playground too long that day. My face was blue and crusty with the cold, and my mother had to bathe my hands in a sink of warm water.

Through all the years of childhood I seemed to know that wherever my father went, there were ladies waiting to draw him even farther away. It made him more precious to me and sharpened my love. But now at nearly fourteen, I'd erased these nameless women from my mind, all except the first one whom I never saw again, the lady in the winter playground, whose laughter spiraled higher than my swing.

Outside my room, the hall was drafty. There were always stray currents running through these rambling rooms. The next door down was the guest room, where my dad had slept before he left. I went in a lot, looking for his traces, but it was all empty drawers and bare hangers. I always left his door open to let my mother know I'd been there.

The living room was a long, low-ceilinged cave, darker than it had been. Once, over the fireplace mantel, my grandmother's picture had hung in a pool of light. It was always called the "Unfinished Portrait of Jessica." I was named for her. At my school there were half a dozen Jessicas, but I was the only one who'd inherited the name. My grandmother had come to this apartment as a bride when the building was the newest, grandest on the Drive, and my dad had grown up here.

She was only this picture to me, and it was a valuable one. My grandmother's brother, Lucius Pirie, had been a painter of beautiful women. She was young when he'd painted her. Her hair was brush strokes of silver-blond and her dress a cool pillar of ice-blue. A long string of pearls hung to her waist, where her hand toyed with them, her fingernails silvery among the pale pearls. When I was little, I'd studied the picture to see if the hand might move in the circle of light in that dim room.

It was called an unfinished portrait, but that made it better. Her hands were beautifully complete, and her face, too, but she seemed to stand against space. The background hadn't been filled in, and she seemed to rise out of clouds, which added to her mystery. At the bottom was Lucius Pirie's signature, scrawled as if in haste.

It was said he'd gone away without finishing it, giving up his career of painting beautiful society women in search of something else. He seemed to go just in time, leaving things about her to your imagination. He'd put diamonds in her ears before he left. It's hard to paint diamonds, but I knew the earrings; my mother wore them later because Grandmother Ferris had left them to her.

The picture was gone now. My father had left in August, but he came back for it. I was home one afternoon just before school started when the phone rang. It was Dad, and I had him back with me for a moment, his voice. He seemed to know my mother was out. She'd had the locks changed, but I was here, her eager enemy within the gates.

He came with a carrying case for the picture and some of the things he needed. I thought that he might take me too. Wasn't I something he needed? He'd called from a phone on Rush Street, and in the time it took him to get here, I had a dream of packing, of throwing some clothes into a backpack and going with him—wherever. I couldn't breathe with thinking about that when the bell rang, and he stood there filling up the door.

"Jess," he said, and I thought my heart was going to burst open. Even before, he'd been away a lot. He wasn't like other people's boring fathers, who went off in the morning in suits and brought work home every night. Black-socked fathers in Brooks Brothers suits, who did things at desks. My dad wore a flight jacket, and when he went away the world stopped, and when he came back, it was worth it. He breezed in—that was the word—and there was the old-leather

scent of his flight jacket, and in his eyes you could
almost see where he'd been, but never quite. Now he
was back again, and yes I could feel my heart bursting
open.

But he couldn't take me. When he left, he went
quickly, moving like a panther or something, looking
at the watch on his square wrist and not at me. I supposed if he had, if our eyes had met, he couldn't have
left me at all.

I stood in the hall with the apartment echoing behind me while the elevator whirred him away, and
the things he'd taken. If he'd packed up everything,
every stick of furniture and the floorboards, I'd have
understood. They were his. Everything about this
place was his. My mother had driven him away, or she
couldn't keep him, which was the same thing.

Later, when she came home, I wasn't in my room as
usual. I was in the living room with a book propped
up in front of me. I wanted to watch her face when
she discovered the picture was gone. She saw at once,
and we were both suspended in the moment when
she realized I'd let him in. I was braced, but she didn't
say anything.

She turned and walked straight into the dining
room, and I heard a drawer open. Then her silence
again. He'd taken the silver. It was the big mahogany
box full of heavy fiddleback spoons and pistol-grip

knives that had been in the Ferris family before the Chicago Fire. My mother and dad were given it on their wedding day, but it was really his. And she'd gone right to the empty drawer. I hated her for that, for knowing him better than—anybody.

Now, these months later, the living room was dark all the way to the wind-rattled windows at the far end. Christmas lights showed in the building across the street. If she—if my mother suggested a tree, I'd decided to say no. This was the first Christmas without Dad, and I wanted it to hurt.

The dining room was darker still. We never ate in there now. A line of light showed under the swing door. Standing with my cheek against the varnished wood, I tried to hear her thoughts before I pushed through into the kitchen.

The ceiling lights bounced off all the white surfaces. She sat bunched in her bathrobe at the table, stirring her cocoa mug with a kitchen spoon. Her hands were slender and tapering, but she kept her nails short. I liked long, shapely fingernails buffed to a dull glow. I bit mine.

She worked at home in an office she'd created out of the maid's room behind the kitchen. There hadn't been a live-in maid since Grandmother Ferris's time. She had a word processor back there and did clerical work for people, answering their mail or something. I didn't know what she did.

The empty chair was too near her. I thought of taking my mug and turning away and walking out of the room, but I wasn't sure I could pull it off. I hovered at my distance, staring down into the mug, feeling her gaze. Behind me the refrigerator hummed, and off to my left was the swing door to freedom. "Christmas," she said. "We need to make some plans about—"

"Rhonda," I said, blurting it out. I'd startled myself into meeting my mother's gaze: blue eyes the color of mine. Rhonda?

I never talked about school. Rhonda was a girl at school. She was the whole school that year as far as our group was concerned. We wore her labels and laughed her laugh. We rallied around Rhonda and took her whims as law. She lived farther up the Drive, in a monstrous new high-rise with floor-to-ceiling windows on the lake and a sunburst chandelier in the lobby and white Lincoln limos in a curving drive.

Their apartment was all white carpeting and lipstick-red upholstery, and Rhonda's mother was as big as a house. Rhonda was a little thick in the waist herself and called anybody thinner "anorexic." We ate hearty at her table in the lunchroom. Where Rhonda was, there was the world.

She was going away at Christmas with her family, to some fabulous place. St. Lucia, I think. Some perfect place, and she'd hinted that she was going to invite one of us to go with her. She'd dropped her hints all fall, and I wanted it to be me. I dreamed about it, there on an endless beach under a white sun, Rhonda's chosen. She knew how to keep us guessing and off-guard, but I must have known that her first choice would be one of the other Jessicas. And her second, Meg. I thought of telling her something nobody else knew—that my dad had left.

But I wouldn't have told that to anybody in the world. Even before Dad left, I'd always been afraid that one day I'd turn around and he'd be gone. By the time he left, I'd already built this shell around myself. A word from anybody could shatter it, and so I never told.

Besides, I must have known that Rhonda had no pity. She was never going to take me to St. Lucia, but I thought I was overdue for a miracle: being in a wonderful Rhonda-kind-of-place while my mother was left alone in these dark rooms beside the frozen lake, at Christmas.

In the end, Rhonda didn't take any of us, but I didn't know that yet. I wasn't quite wise enough to see she'd never intended to.

My mother seemed not to wonder why this Rhonda

person was the only thing in my mind. She was about to announce our Christmas plans, and my flesh crawled. The two of us in this treeless apartment. I could live in my room. I'd been proving that all fall, but Christmas was a longer day. Still, it would be another chance to let her know how much I—

"I'll be going to the Brennans for Christmas Day," she said, crosscutting my thoughts.

I? Had she said _I?_ Where did that leave me? What was I supposed to do? The Brennans lived up in Evanston, with kids coming home from college to a big house surrounded by cars and bikes. A real family. Mrs. Brennan had come a lot to see my mother after Dad left. My mother knew a lot of people. They came around and called up. But Mrs. Brennan seemed to be my mother's best friend. I didn't know. To me, friendship was trying to be Rhonda.

"And then," my mother said, "I'm facing some work deadlines. I'll be working through the holidays." She'd taken off her glasses and pinched the bridge of her nose where the glasses had pinched. The cocoa mug was burning a spot on my knuckle, but I decided to let it.

She ran her hand into the neck of her robe. "I don't know if I'm doing the right thing," she said, "or if I'm doing it for the right reasons." She seemed intent on a corner of the kitchen where nobody was. "How would you like to spend the holidays with your father?"

I managed to set the mug down. For some reason I'd been letting it burn my hand. Cocoa sloshed out and ran down. My heart turned over and thumped at my ribs, trying to get out. I was lighter. I couldn't feel my feet, and Rhonda fled.

It was a miracle. Dad had sent for me, and she couldn't keep us apart. They'd struggled over me behind my back, and he'd won me. Now she was trying to make it sound like her idea, her decision. Let her, as long as—

"I don't think it's a good idea," she said, "but it's the only one I have. We're not getting anywhere on our own, you and I. You're trying to live in your room, and I don't think it's working very well for you."

But I hardly heard her because the miracle was unfolding all around me. Everywhere I looked was Dad's face, almost in focus.

"It's a long way," she said quietly.

I didn't know where Dad was, but she wasn't supposed to know that. She was supposed to think that I got letters from him, addressed to me at school or somewhere. She was to think that he called me up whenever she was out. Once when I'd heard her key in the door, I raced to the hall phone and then hung up just as she came in. But she didn't ask me who it was. She was supposed to think I knew every step he'd taken since the—separation.

I didn't know if it was a divorce. There'd been lawyers, but if she had any legal rights, I didn't want to hear them. After the day I'd let Dad in to take away the painting and the other things, I pulled farther back from her. I knew I'd betrayed her, but it was her fault.

"I wish you weren't hurting like this," she said. She put out her hand, reached out toward me. But between us was the table, and everything. "It's come at a bad time for you," she said, bringing up a sigh. "I see that now."

I couldn't even think what she was talking about. It couldn't have come at a better time. It was Christmas vacation, and I'd be with Dad.

Then I saw she meant their breakup, but I was lucky he hadn't left her long ago. He would have, if it hadn't been for me.

"Still, if he'd stayed longer," she said, "it would have been harder for you."

"Harder?" I said, breaking through my silence. How could anything be harder than these past months?

"In time you'd have seen through him," she said. "People do."

I'd heard enough now. I turned to the door, making a pact with myself. I'd never let myself be as bitter as she was, not after I got away from her. My mind was already skipping ahead. I was going to be with Dad at Christmas, and that would be the first step away from her and this empty apartment and being not-quite-fourteen and all the hours that had to be filled. One day I'd have him, and she wouldn't.

I was at the door now but she spoke behind me. "Another mistake your dad and I made. We should have fought more in front of you, where you could see. Then it wouldn't all have been such a shock to you. But he was away so much, wasn't he?"

He was away on location for his photography. He was in New York getting together a gallery show of his pictures. He was gone because he didn't want to be with her. It wasn't his fault.

"I didn't know you'd be so hurt about losing something you never had," Mom said. That pushed me to the edge and almost over. There was a sob inside me, rising, a sob I meant to keep from her. Nobody was supposed to see me cry, especially—

"Now he's in Mexico," she said. "At his Uncle Lucius's house, so at least you'll have a place to stay."

What was that supposed to mean? I swallowed hard. Wouldn't I have a place to stay wherever Dad was? Just because he wasn't still here under her thumb like I was, did that mean he was in some mission for homeless men or something? Some shelter? Couldn't the earth turn without her?

Mexico: I saw this unknown place alive and beckoning across the blank door to the dining room. Endless beach under a white sun. I saw Dad and me, only the two of us in the world, walking along the beach, and my profile was turned up to him. We walked hand in hand, and I felt the grit of sand in his strong grip and the cool surf between my toes as it scalloped the sand. I felt Mexico warm on my face and tried to erase the days between.

CHAPTER 2

SHE'D SENT FOR A CAB, AND THE DOORMAN, Vince, came up for my things. I wasn't taking a lot because I was going to the sun, and when I got there I'd be someone else.

I was layered, and on top I had a Guess? Windbreaker and a wool scarf wound around my neck. Underneath everything, next to my skin, a secret wallet hung from a cord around my neck. I was carrying my traveler's checks in it and plenty of Mexican pesos and a Xerox copy of my birth certificate in case I had to show it. She'd made me wear this thing, and now I could hear her thinking that I'd lose it.

In the lobby Vince said it was eighteen degrees outside. The wind off the lake made ice sculptures of the stop sign and the fire hydrant. I was already on my way now. I'd taken the first steps, but change scared me, even this one. I thought about going back up in the elevator for one more look at my room. Something seemed to be pulling me back. I shot my mother a sharp look to make sure it wasn't her. The cab wheeled up outside, throwing black slush.

I put my flight bag on the backseat between us. She was too near, and her perfume filled the cab. She was different outside the apartment. I didn't go anywhere with her anymore, and I'd trained her to stay away from anything at school. But when she wasn't wearing her thinking-woman's bathrobe, she was taller, narrower. She loosened her cherry-red wool coat, and it fell open to show the Magnin's label. "If you need more money . . ." But I was looking away from her, watching my breath on the window.

Why a money lecture, when it all came from Dad somehow anyway? Even the apartment we lived in came from him and his family. He was the source of everything. Why did she always try to make herself so important, when she wasn't? The trip out to O'Hare was going to be endless. The cab threaded through the sleety streets, nowhere near the expressway yet, and the crosswalks were full of Christmas shoppers.

That made me think of earlier Christmases. My mother had taken me in my leggings to Marshall

Field's, down on State Street, to have lunch in the Walnut Room around the tree and to see Santa. I remembered the long line of mothers and children moving up on Santa's throne. Huge Santa with that flowing beard and those big blob boots and that blinding red suit—terrifying and traditional. We went every year until the Santa magic melted.

My mother said something, and I was so lost in thought that I turned to her. "What?"

"Marshall Field's," she said, "and the tree and Santa Claus."

I wondered if I'd ever be free of her and the way she couldn't leave my thoughts alone. I unzipped the flight bag and took out my book, *Love's Incandescence,* and tried to find my place in it.

There was another long wait in the boarding lounge with nowhere to sit. Time crept. We listened to piped-in airport Christmas music.

"As soon as you get there, put your return ticket in a safe place," she said, while I stood there dreaming of never coming back. "And be careful of the water. Don't drink it. The one thing you don't want is to be sick down there."

Because nobody would take care of me, I supposed.

"If nobody's at the airport to meet you—"

"He'll be there," I said.

Then we were staring at our feet. She was wearing

her boots with the heels, Charles Jourdan, left over from her marriage. I was wearing status sneakers and big Day-Glo pink socks. A fad for Day-Glo pink had swept the school, and Rhonda had okayed it. Finally people began lining up for the gate. "You don't have to wait any longer," I said past her.

From the corner of my eye I saw her smile, a smile from some earlier time. "Don't tempt me," she said.

They called the flight, and people were hoisting their carry-on bags. I propped my book under my arm. "The plane makes a stop in Houston, but don't get off there," she said, a parting shot. Then when I thought the line might move and she'd go away, she spoke my name.

I looked back at her. We hadn't touched because she didn't want me pulling back from her in public.

"You don't have to," she said, holding her coat tight around her, though it was hot in here. "You could come home and we . . . You don't have to go."

I looked away so she couldn't see my eyes. She knew any change, anything different scared me. She was using that.

"I said something to you the other night I'm sorry about, Jessica." The line of people was only jostling, not moving, and I didn't know how much more of this I could take. "I said if your dad had stayed longer, you'd have seen through him, because people do. I shouldn't have said that. It doesn't do any good, and it's the kind of thing you can say to another adult, not a child. Forget it."

"I already have," I said, and now the line moved, and I walked away from her, to him.

At the end of the runway the plane lingered, while gray snow slanted past the windows. If we chanced a take-off at all, I thought the lake wind would sweep us out of the sky. I had a clear vision of us being rained over the Chicago Loop in a hail of plane parts and seats we were still strapped into, and Mexican pesos. I was trapped in a window seat of a plane fatally over-loaded with people's Christmas presents they'd never live to give and coats we wouldn't need where we were going. I would die before high school. Panic rose in my throat. Then I was blazing mad at having to risk my life to be with Dad. If it hadn't been for—

The plane lurched and lumbered, gathering sickening speed. Then we were tearing through layers of weather. I was clinging to *Love's Incandescence* as if it alone could keep us in the air. My fingers left smudge marks on the book's slick paper jacket. Angela Chatsworth's picture wasn't on the back cover, so I didn't even have her for company. I sat rigid for hours, years, and then disappeared into the story, committing whole passages to memory.

_She knew that the danger lay ahead, not behind. She
looked back to see the prim safety of all that she had
known and been, at the thousand-year history of her family, the MacLarens, and of their noble house, Loch
Melfort. No, the danger lay ahead, in leaving all that she
had known among these Scottish hills to follow where her
lover led. There lay the danger. She saw it in his
eyes. . . ._

I remembered not to get off when we landed at
Houston, the last stop this side of the border. After
that I slept, cramped in the seat with the wallet's sharp
corners digging into my skin, under the clothes.
There wasn't anything to see out the window anyway.
I was over the wing.

Then an announcement woke me up, and the plane
was full of afternoon light. It felt warm at the window, another time of year. It was Mexico as we
slanted in: vague sea off to one side and brown earth
below, and I wasn't sure if I was awake or not.

There were barriers you had to get through, and
the airport here was colder than O'Hare, summery,
air-conditioned air. Already, I was looking for him
among the faces.

People held up signs with names on them—limo
drivers and hotel vans. I was in this funnel of people,
and we were past all the barriers, and still he wasn't

here. When the crowds thinned, it was worse. I thought I might be left standing here alone. And I didn't see Dad. It wasn't the two of us. It was the one of me, the way it always . . .

Two people were standing there, and maybe they'd been there all along. A guy and a girl, young, though not as young as I was. She was beautiful: tall and slender with dark hair and a heart-shaped face. She wore a long cotton skirt, no color, and sandals that wrapped up around her ankles. She had on a sleeveless blouse and a long silver chain around her neck.

And he was even better. He wore running shorts and a bright shirt, and he was barefoot. His sunglasses kept me from seeing his eyes, but hers were almost green. I noticed that much because she had a terrific tan, dark and even. He was blond and burned, with a peeling nose. I didn't think they were quite real. They were that perfect. Across a little distance she said, "Are you Jessica Ferris?"

I'd been saved.

"Welcome to Acapulco," he said, this wonderful-looking blond guy, and he reached out and put a hand on my shoulder, which was somehow the perfect greeting. "Where'd you come from, the Klondike?"

The three of us made our way through the airport. She was telling him that he'd parked in the wrong place. We waited for my suitcase, she and I, while he went off to see about his car. I was so dazzled that I wasn't even thinking about Dad.

"My name is Brooke McMillan," she said. McMillan was a Scottish name. She was exactly like the girl, the young woman in the book I was reading.

"And his name is Tony Rhodes."

"Are you . . ." I didn't know what I was going to ask. In a wonderful gesture, Brooke swept her hair back. It was long and very dark and fell lower than her shoulders. She had a collection of square, silver-wire bracelets that clattered with a little sound on her arm.

"I'm staying at the house with you, at your great-uncle's house. I'm one of the house party. My aunt and I are."

A house party like they had in books: wonderful, unreal people who came to stay in fabulous houses. "It'll be fun," she said, as if I were her age.

I wondered if they . . .

"Tony's there, too, staying in the *caseta* at the end of the garden. He's in college. He'll probably tell you he's a dropout, but he's down here doing an independent study."

"Are you in college?" I asked her. She must be. She was so . . .

"Not yet. I'm taking a year off, after Chapin."

I knew about Chapin. It was the best girls' school in New York, for the best girls. The school I went to called itself "The Chicago Chapin."

"My dad," I said.

"You'll see him after we get home."

Then I understood what he'd done, and it was perfect. Instead of meeting me himself, he'd sent Brooke and Tony so I'd have friends, young ones, right from the start. They weren't as young as I was, which wouldn't have been perfect. They were older, like I wanted to be. They weren't even in school. They were freer than that.

My suitcase was coming down the conveyor belt. Tony was back, reaching past me for it. Through one more pair of doors we were outside, and the heat hit us. A man with a face like a brown nut under a big hat, a sombrero, was selling things to wear, woven out of strings. Next to him a woman in shapeless clothes with her hair in a braid held out her dusty hand, begging. The heat was breathtaking.

Tony's car was outside, with one wheel up on the crumbling sidewalk. It was the weirdest car I'd ever seen: no roof, no doors, and cut-down corrugated metal sides painted the same color as my socks. He did a wild dance around it with my suitcase as partner, because his feet were bare on the broiling pavement.

I went in the back, and we sorted out headgear

because he said we had to cover our heads in this sun. His was a ballcap that he slapped on backward, street-gang style. The others were straw. Brooke fished one up and put it on all in a single gesture. It was wide in the brim and turned up in front with a funny paper rose there. When she turned back to me, she looked like a high-fashion model in a thousand-dollar hat. I found one with a hole in the crown and a curly brim, which was all right because I couldn't compete with Brooke. I must have looked like Mary Poppins at puberty, but when Tony turned around, he blinked and then said, "Great. And unwind the scarf. We're talking tropics here."

We gunned away in this go-to-the-beach car in our hats, bobbing and weaving through traffic that didn't play by the rules. There were mountains on one side and the hazy sea on the other. It was like the first day of summer, but better, and somehow stolen.

The roadside was full of people and stands selling things, and the hulks of stripped cars. When Tony turned off the highway, we hit bottom and bounced on a dirt road. It looped like a dry river bed, but we were getting nearer the ocean. The clay turned sandy, and there were huge rocks and wandering fences and the shapes of things I'd never seen growing before, shapes like giant asparagus.

The road dipped into little twilights and back up

again. Just as it seemed to crest one last hill with the
sea low on the other side, Tony swung the car up to a
big wooden gate in a long, uneven wall. He climbed
out to push the buttons in a metal box. We were outside some private world. As the dust settled around
us, I sat looking at Brooke's graceful arm, where it
rested across the back of Tony's seat.

That was the first time I came to the house that was
called *Amor y Muerte*. My great-uncle had built it up in
the rocks, facing west so that it turned its eyes to the
sea. The lane leading from the gate climbed through
collapsed arbors. Dusty hedges became walls, and the
walls became outbuildings that rose to a house, like a
village jumbled together.

Trees sheltered the slants of roof. They were banana trees and sapodilla, looking like enormous potted plants. But it was the bougainvillea I noticed first.
It smothered the windows and reached across the
eaves. It was in December bloom, an intense rose-
purple. We pulled up in a circle that turned around a
rusted sundial. The sea lay below, and miles out it was
dark in the dipping sun.

Brooke led me, and I entered in a trance, looking
for my father around every corner. Hadn't I always?
And there were a lot of corners here. Narrow halls
ran everywhere. Sometimes the walls were the raw
rocks the house was built among.

She showed me to my room. Its tiled floors were swept, not scrubbed. Even now the rasp of sand on a floor takes me back there. It seemed bare at first. Only a few pieces of old Mexican furniture. The walls were networked with cracks. There was a mirror in a tin frame, and in a niche a wooden carving of a saint and a votive light with the candle burned away. In an Angela Chatsworth novel there'd be French doors opening onto a marble balcony. Here was just an opening onto an earth-floored clearing with a path leading away. The house had been built without thought of air-conditioning, and so there was no clear division between indoor and out. There was nothing very clear about it.

Outside, you could look down the rocky cliffs all the way to the bay, and to a rickety pier out into the water. Down a few wide steps from the house a long terrace surrounded a swimming pool. Big earthen pots of some intense red flower stood at all four corners of it.

The colors were all brilliant, even the sky, and they pulled at my eyes after the drab Chicago winter. A woman sat beside the pool in a long chair, with one arm resting on the low adobe wall. She looked out at the fiery dust ball of a sun, which was just beginning to balance on the horizon. She sat so quietly calm that I hadn't seen her at first. She'd been swimming. Now she wore a long cover-up that fell open to show the length of her leg. I couldn't see her face, and I didn't wait for her to move. I turned back into the room that was darker now.

There was a picture on the wall, a small one in a raw wood frame. It was a painting of a woman: only her head, with a loose shawl thrown over it, and you were very close to her, or rather the painter was. She was Mexican in her eyes and cheekbones, and even in the colors of the shawl and the triangles of sky behind her.

When I looked around, she was standing in the door. The sight stunned me. It was the same woman in the picture, though she wasn't wearing the shawl. In the picture you could see in the length of her face that she was a big woman. In real life she was as tall as the door. Her cheekbones were high and her eyes absolutely black—flat black eyes, with maybe only a glint of curiosity behind them. Though she should have been wearing some exotic costume, it was a white nylon uniform, which zipped up. In her hands was a pile of towels. Without a word, she showed me to the bathroom, and disappeared into the mystery of the house.

The bathroom was larger than my room, with a square tub set into the floor. Once, you could have walked down the steps to have your bath there. But the faucets were capped, and the dry bottom was webbed and looked spidery. There was a functional-looking sink, and as an afterthought a sheet-metal shower stall in the corner.

I stood under the stuttering water while the dust ran off me in rivers. With a bar of soap I scrubbed my hair before I realized there'd be no hair drier.

In my room, in the bathrobe my mother had remembered to pack for me, I worked over my hair. There was something familiar about this unknown place. I couldn't think what, at first. It was the sand underfoot and the summery heat and the outdoor smells of growing things. It reminded me of the summer I'd gone to camp. I was ten, and I hated being away, for fear my dad would leave while I was gone— or come back when I wasn't home. Something like that. The whole time at camp, my throat had been tight. It was tightening again now, and I was beginning to panic. Outside, only the light had changed. The sea was green until the horizon, where the sun had seemed to singe it in setting. Down at the pool the woman still sat in the long chair, possibly waiting.

A man was coming down from the house to her. He was old as the hills, even from this distance, and very heavy. He took the steps one at a time, fishing for the next one with his foot. Beside him someone slim, all in white, helped him along. They moved in slow motion. Before they reached the swimming-pool terrace, the woman looked away from the sea to them and put out her hand.

But I didn't have time for her. Something moved in the seascape far below. Down by the pier a little boat like a knife was drawing in. Somebody jumped across and secured it. They were fishermen bringing in their catch, two or three of them setting a big basket of flopping fish on the pier.

I threw down the towel and began to run. There was a path and steps and then a fork in the path. One way led to the swimming pool; the other went steeper down past cactus clinging to the cliffs. The path became wooden slats, and they became the pier, and I was running flat out in my flapping bathrobe. Because it was my dad stepping across onto the pier now, with the sunset in his hair, reaching for a shirt to pull on over his big shoulders. Now he saw me stumbling along with my hair on end, ready to break my neck to be there. It was my dad, like a god from the sea.

CHAPTER 3

IT WASN'T HOW I THOUGHT IT WOULD BE. I'D thought it would be the two of us.

At dinner that night we sat six at the table, with my great-uncle, Lucius Pirie, at the head. The house wasn't really as random as the rocks. It had been built according to several plans. Some of it surrounded a courtyard, a long generous room without floor or roof. We dined that first night in this secret garden, under stars.

I was exhausted by then, and confused. I didn't even understand the food. But Dad had caught the fish, so they were delicious.

Did I understand that this great-uncle was Lucius Pirie, the once-famous artist who'd painted the por-

trait of my grandmother? He'd seated me at his right,
a place of honor. I'd never been near anyone as old,
or as big. He wore a vast Mexican shirt embroidered
white-on-white. His face was all folds and sagging circles. He seemed like an enormous frog who'd ar-
ranged the rest of us on his lily pad.

Even if I could have read his eyes, they were invisible behind round spectacle rims that added two more
circles to his face. Behind him in shadow stood the
young man who'd helped him down the steps. He
stood there through the evening, statue-still, in a uniform glowing like phosphorous, not waiting on us,
only attending Lucius Pirie.

The tall woman, Blanca, whose face hung in my
room, served us. Her long hands moved in between
us as she went about her work. Occasionally Lucius
Pirie made a small gesture meant for her, but usually
she moved just ahead of his needs. At first I wondered
if he was too old to speak. His breath came short and
wheezy.

Candles burned in big glass chimneys the same
color as the sea. We sat in the pools of this underwater
light, and the conversation came and went in waves.
Tony sat on my other side, wearing a spanking white
tuxedo shirt with a red bow tie. No coat, of course,
and white pants rolled to the knee.

Opposite me, on Lucius Pirie's other side, was

Brooke. Her smiles across at Tony and me were candlelit, and she wore a flower in her hair, an hibiscus. It knocked me out. I wanted one in mine.

At the far end Brooke's aunt sat, Margo Warner, the woman who'd been sitting beside the pool. She and Brooke were dressed in the same way, in saris of a sort that wrapped around, leaving their shoulders bare. Brooke's was a tissue silk almost orange, wonderful with her greenish eyes. Her aunt wore lemon-yellow with a green orchid she might have picked off a vine and then pinned there between her breasts. Their wraps became evening gowns here at the table, where nothing was quite real. I wanted a wrap, something clinging, and wished I had something for it to cling to. Brooke's aunt reminded me of someone, I couldn't think who.

My dad sat at an angle across from me, two candles away. His hair was a mass of curls tightened by sun and sea. He looked as young as Tony. I kept seeing Dad in profile as he turned toward Margo, Brooke's aunt, listening to her. Once in a while he looked down the table and grinned at me, expanding his eyes as if he couldn't believe I was really here at last.

On the pier when we'd met, there'd been a perfect moment when he'd hugged me and swung me in the air. I was too old for that, but it was where I'd always wanted to be. Now at the table I concentrated on him, willing him to look my way more often.

But conversations kept flowing between us, and they'd all begun before I'd come. Tony and Brooke talked across the table to each other as if you didn't need to be careful about what adults heard. I didn't know what to think.

Even the cutlery worried me. I wasn't sure which knives and forks and spoons to use as the courses came and went. Tony noticed. I looked down to find I had even more spoons than before. I was up to four where there'd been just three. Then in a blink I had five, and Tony's hand was just retreating. He was teasing me out of my dilemma by adding his spoons to mine. I didn't get it at first. Then with one eye on me, he speared at his salad with two forks fitted together. Across the candlelight Brooke was swallowing laughter. But I wasn't used to it, and I wondered if he and Brooke . . .

"For dessert there'll be flan," Tony said out of the corner of his mouth. "Kind of a caramel custard. Use the big spoon at the top of the plate. Otherwise we fling you into a volcano as a sacrificial maiden. It's one of our Aztec traditions."

"Oh," I said, brilliantly.

Still I willed Dad to look my way. But he was turned to Margo Warner, who was talking to him about the quality of Mexican light, whatever that meant. He was nodding, perhaps looking past her into the rooms around us, where paintings hung in spots of soft light.

Lucius Pirie spoke then, in a voice that rang like a bell from a distant tower. He was terrifying. He was speaking to me.

"By rights, there should be a well here in the dead center of the courtyard, if this were in truth a Mexican house and not one of my pastiches. By rights you, young lady, should be sitting with your feet dangling down a well. It would be the center of everything in an authentic Mexican house."

"Like 'The Well at Casa Felipe,' " Tony said to him, coming to my rescue. Lucius Pirie nodded, pleased. In a voice the old man could hear, Tony said to me, "Lucius Pirie did a series of oils of traditional Mexican houses when he first came to this country. There was a show of them in Chicago—"

"And another in London," Lucius Pirie remarked.

"They caused a tremendous sensation," Tony said. "Nobody'd seen anything like them—that quality of Mexican light."

"My early period," Lucius Pirie said. Now he was a vast volcano, coming rumblingly alive at the top. "When Mexico was Mexico. There wouldn't have been ten thousand souls in Acapulco then, not that I came to Acapulco. Nobody did. I knew D. H. Lawrence, you know."

I didn't know that, or D. H. Lawrence. I was sinking fast, because I wasn't used to sitting at a dinner table with older people. I was used to sitting in my room, thinking how mature I was. Tony leaned nearer, almost past me, with his hand braced on the back of my chair. We were cheek-to-cheek as he hung on every word the old man said.

"Dreadful little man, was Lawrence, and wrote the most cloying claptrap about Mexico. He was English, you see, and the English never really leave home, do they? Everywhere they look it's either England or their hatred of England. And that awful German wife he had, if wife she was."

Tony was inhaling every word. I hadn't put it together, but it was obvious. Tony's independent project for his winter term in Mexico was Lucius Pirie. And Tony was serious about it. He practically had a tape recorder on his knee. It was strange. Lucius Pirie was the great-uncle I'd hardly known I had, and Tony had come all this way to sit at his feet and study him like a class.

"My early period," Lucius Pirie said again. Now we were all listening. "1927." He looked around the table, and behind his spectacles I think he blinked. Nobody else at the table had been born for years after that—decades. He sighed slightly, and then went back to D. H. Lawrence, this bad writer with the awful wife.

"He'd come to Mexico hoping to find a climate he could live in. Futile, of course. People ought not to come to Mexico to live. It's a place to die."

There was a sudden stillness around the table. Lucius Pirie was ninety, at least.

Margo Warner spoke from the other end of the table, lightly touching the orchid she wore. "But surely you didn't come here in 1927 to die, Lucius."

He put his head back and seemed to see her from under his glasses. "You know me, Margo. I always plan ahead. We're alike, you and I. We make long plans and nobody gets in our way. We look at the big picture."

There was a murmur of laughter then. Maybe there was a pun in "big picture."

But now, more terror. Lucius Pirie turned to me and touched my hand with his. It was enormous and very pale. He wore a ring with a turquoise bigger than a robin's egg, set in silver. "I didn't begin this house until after the war. The war made Acapulco, you know. The rich couldn't get to Europe, and so they came here. They built a resort from a fishing village, and a city from a resort."

"But never an artists' colony," Brooke said, and he

turned to her in a way that gathered her in. She looked like her aunt, and he liked her aunt.

"No, Acapulco was never much of an artists' colony. But an artist doesn't have to live with other artists. An artist needs buyers for his work. Talent may happen to anyone, but you must have a plan. An artist needs clients with money so new that they will buy good work to prove the taste they don't yet have. That's the artist's need—that and keeping the critics off-balance."

Margo laughed, a handful of musical notes, and maybe that meant Lucius Pirie wasn't being serious. I couldn't tell.

I thought that Dad would look at me again, while the conversation between Lucius Pirie and Brooke's aunt played back and forth like table tennis. I could see that Dad had by far the best tan at the table, and he was shaggier now. This wasn't haircut country, of course. He'd grown a mustache, which had tickled me when he'd kissed me down at the pier. His shagginess somehow made him handsomer. But different, too, less like all my pictures of him, and I had this problem about change. But there was still that same long distance in his eyes. I supposed he was visualizing photographs he wanted to take, maybe the perfect photograph, ideally lit and composed. After all, there was this artistic strain that ran through the family.

Then Tony said to me, "Margo Warner owns one of the best art galleries in New York." I looked at her again. She, too, wore a ring on her right hand, a magnificent aquamarine an inch long, in a bed of diamonds.

"No, Lucius, tell us what brought you first to Mexico," she said, "truly." Perhaps she was asking so Tony could hear.

"I came," Lucius Pirie said in his hollow voice, "because all the colors there are meet in Mexico. I came knowing that one day they were bound to converge finally in some great cleansing explosion. I await it hourly."

Then like a bad movie, the candle nearest him guttered and went dead, dimming his spectacles.

He was too old to stay up late, and I barely made it through the flan. I was asleep almost before I found my bed. It was narrow, with tall posts swagged in mosquito netting. I slept beneath dreaming and awoke in the middle of the night, not knowing where I was. I thought I was cold, but it was the clamminess of the sea in a thin layer over lingering heat. I was in a cocoon of mosquito netting that made the rest of the room a ghost. Then I heard, again, the sound that must have awakened me.

A pair of voices sounded, murmuring words I couldn't hear. There was the sound of water, too, not the sea, a sound as sensuous as skin. And from some-where farther off around the bay, distant music. I lay there pinned down by fatigue, and heard two people in the swimming pool speaking quietly, intimately, swimming lazily. I listened to their rhythms until they lulled me back to sleep.

When I awoke again, the morning was slipping away, and I wasn't alone in the bed. A dog was taking up most of it with her heavy, sleeping head on my feet. She was the color of a fawn, but bigger—a mas-tiff, or something. Her name was Luna, and she and her brothers and sisters patrolled the grounds at night and were allowed to sleep during the day, anywhere they liked. I learned that from Brooke, who was standing at the foot of the bed.

She was in a halter top that showed a bare, narrow middle. Her hair was brushed back and tied with a thong. She was old enough not to mind looking younger, and now she knotted the mosquito netting around the bed posts. The silver bracelets sang on her arms. "It's late," she said. "Don't sleep it all away."

I was wearing an infantile pair of pajamas that made me want to clutch the sheet to my chin, if I could get it away from Luna. "And anyway," Brooke was say-ing, "it's banana-boat day, which is a hoot."

I didn't know what that meant. "Dad—" I said.

"He and Margo went over early to the Princess Hotel to get in some tennis before it's really hot."

"Why?"

She looked at me with her eyebrows high on her forehead. "Because there isn't a tennis court here. Come on. We're going to take you into town. You have to see it, and anyway you'll want to get a swimsuit. Anything you bought last summer probably won't do now."

That was true. Last summer I had even less shape, and nothing I'd brought was right for here.

"Did you bring money or plastic?"

"Yes," I said. "My mother . . . yes."

"Tony's cranking up his car. Give you five minutes, if you can do without breakfast." She went out through the porch, and I watched the light capture her, the Mexican light. I wished it was me I was watching.

We barreled off down the dust-bowl road in our headgear. Today, Tony's was a giveaway cap featuring a raffia chicken with real pinfeathers stapled to the bill. We bounced away, and it was almost perfect.

The house was half a dozen bays away from Acapulco, and the coastal highway began to climb and reach around a high headland. Now we were above the roadside slums and the Pemex gas stations. We were swooping through a neighborhood of villas with long, dramatic drops and artificial waterfalls. We came around the headland, and now the tour buses were lumbering all around us, and there was this sense of something wonderful about to happen.

Manuevering madly, Tony swerved off the road and stopped. Above us was Las Brisas Hotel, rising in clouds of bougainvillea and hibiscus. Here between the highway and the drop to the sea was a little place where you could stand under trees that framed a view.

We were high at one end of a bay that swept for miles around in a giant question mark. It was dotted with yachts, and the city strung around it like diamonds around an aquamarine. Everywhere in the skies were the colored mushrooms of the parasailors, dangling barefoot far above the beaches. "This is the best moment," Brooke said.

Tony nodded. He stood between us with his arms around our shoulders. "It tends to be all downhill from here."

We descended into glitzy, gritty Acapulco and shopped the morning away. The malls blasted air-conditioning and the air outside was oven-hot and full of fumes. By lunchtime we were around an umbrella table at a place called Paradise. It was a bar and terrace restaurant between the bayside boulevard, the Costera, and the beach. To get in, we'd had to pass the beggars—children begging, with smaller children slung on their backs in sarapes. Children begging for money, with their small hands out.

But inside, it was Paradise, or near enough. The dance floor was jammed with bronzed bodies at high noon, pumping to a furious lambada. The beach itself was standing-room-only, right down to the water's edge. But nobody was swimming because of the sewage. The waiters were all stars, and they brought us leis to wear because this was supposed to be Hawaii as well as Mexico, or any paradise you wanted. It was a dream world, for the young and nobody else. On the dance floor the girls threw their manes of hair, and the guys rippled in their tanktops, and the music pounded so you were dancing even sitting at the table.

Tony ordered for us: crepés de chuitlacoche, which I ate before I found out they were corn-fungus pancakes, and mineral water with the cap still on the bottle because Brooke insisted.

By then I was in a Poco-Loco T-shirt. In the matching Poco-Loco beach bag was a new Ellesse swimsuit that I wouldn't have had the nerve to buy except for Brooke. Even Tony had shopped and was wearing a new shirt from Aca-Joe printed all over weirdly with ears of bright yellow corn. He said it went with his chicken cap, which hung on the back of the chair. His sunglasses were propped up in his blond hair, and he was observing the scene around our table with his muscular arms folded across his chest. Brooke wore her hat with the paper rose.

I wondered about them. They'd met the week before, when Brooke and Margo had arrived for Christmas. What had happened between them in that week? They matched: Tony, California-casual. Brooke, New York-sure. Both of them cool beyond my dreams of coolness. I wanted to be both of them.

When the deejay took a break, we could talk. Tony spoke of Lucius Pirie and painting, and then he was less kicked back, more focused. I'd never heard people talk about paintings as if they were living things. Tony and Brooke talked about composition and perspective, the layering of the pigment on the canvas, and always about the quality of light.

Both of Brooke's parents were teachers in an overseas school, so she'd lived with Margo Warner to go to Chapin. Now Brooke was working in her aunt's gallery for a year before college. It was the New York gallery where Lucius Pirie's paintings were sold whenever they came on the market. But none of them had, for years, and he had long since ceased to paint.

"Lucius Pirie never sold out to the abstract expressionists," Tony was saying. "He was above movements, and he's weathered the storms. Now we're on the threshold of a big breakthrough in his reputation."

"But does he care?" Brooke asked. The chain around her neck today was gold, like a long neon loop of sunlight.

"I doubt if he does, but he won't live to see it. His death will trigger a rediscovery, the usual pattern in the politics of art."

"And the business," Brooke said. Maybe the art gallery would be hers one day, and she'd be Margo.

I began to work up a little Harlequin-style romance about Brooke, the gallery owner, and Tony, the art historian. But I was no Angela Chatsworth, and I didn't like my romance story. I couldn't think of a part in it for me.

Anyway, they were talking too much about Lucius Pirie and his genius, and it didn't seem fair. "My dad's a photographer," I said, dropping this into the conversation like a brick.

Brooke nodded. "He's been after Aunt Margo for ages to give his work a New York show."

For ages? Then why didn't she give him a show?

Now that we weren't talking about Lucius Pirie, Tony was looking around for the waiter. But Brooke did something I hardly saw. Her hand was on the table, and it just moved to touch Tony's, a slight signal. "Your dad's good?" she said, to humor me. "A good photographer?"

"Yes. Too good for Chicago. They don't understand him."

"And your mother? What's she like?"

What did she have to do with anything? "She's not . . . creative."

They were both listening to me then, Tony too. "Then how did your parents meet?"

I didn't know what that had to do with anything, but I liked it that they were listening. "In college," I said. "Dad didn't finish because photographers don't have to. But they met at Northwestern when they were both working on the yearbook. Dad did the photography for it. I don't know what my mother did."

Then the check came, and the prices on it had all these zeros like the prices for the clothes we'd bought because there are thousands of Mexican pesos to the dollar. "My treat," Tony said. "Let's consider this a date."

"You can't date us both." Brooke gave him a sultry eyelash look from under her paper rose.

"Sure I can," he said. "I'm from L.A."

That was the banana-boat afternoon. I changed into the new swimsuit in my room, with Brooke there for moral support. It was a blue-green to set off the tan I didn't have yet, and pretty skimpy. If it wasn't the *Sports Illustrated* swimsuit issue, it was getting there. But was I? I liked it though. I liked the feel of it, and me in it, and when I turned to Brooke, she nodded just once, and I knew it was all right. I glanced down, and a lot of me was on display, but Brooke said, "Yes, absolutely." I loved that moment, and her.

She was sensational in a no-nonsense black Lycra from Ocean Pacific that showed very little and promised a lot. We wore big T-shirts down to the pier, where Tony met us. There was just a little sandy area, not a beach. When Brooke and I pulled our T-shirts over our heads, Tony let himself keel over backwards into the sand, knocked out by the sight of us.

The banana boat came—this huge plastic banana shape, yellow trimmed in black. It was a big, bobbing, air-filled shape being pulled by a motorboat. Tony waved it into our pier. You sat on it, straddling it like a horse, and there was room enough for a dozen riders. It was like the world's largest toy. There were kids on it already, most of them younger.

The trick was getting on. You couldn't just step from the pier onto it. But somehow we made it, Tony too, and the boat towed us away, out into the bay. The kids were funny, screaming their heads off and having a great time. I didn't know if it was safe or not.

I kept thinking I'd fall off, but didn't. Anywhere but Mexico we'd have had to wear life jackets.

We were greased with suntan lotion and had zinc oxide on our noses. It was a killer sun, but our feet were in the water, and out in the bay it was a different world. Lucius Pirie's house crouched among the rocks, and all the deep overhangs were dark, like empty eye sockets. We made big circles and picked up more kids from other piers. I was amazed at how much more impressive the other houses were. They were newer, of course. He'd been the first one to build here. But they were grander, walled away from each other with elaborate surveillance devices monitoring their perimeters and satellite dishes like huge mushrooms all over the hillsides. Some of the houses were palaces with statues white as salt and pink domes and elaborate yachts drawn up to fancy piers. The banana boat was there for entertaining the children of those houses. "Who are these people?" I asked over Brooke's shoulder.

"Drug money," she said.

We were out longer than we should have been. I could feel the sun on parts of me the sun had never seen before. But it was awesome, like riding some slick sea monster around a travel-poster bay.

When they towed us back to our pier, the sun was in the west. We had to fall off to get off, and we swam ourselves cool because our bay wasn't polluted. When we came up the steps to the swimming-pool terrace, a table was set for tea. The wind fluttered the hem of the white cloth, and the red sun played off the silver tea things. Margo Warner sat at the table. Still there was something familiar about her.

She was passing a plate of cakes to Dad, their hands meeting. He sat near her, his shirt open down his chest, his long legs in immaculate white slacks, his feet crossed at bare, brown ankles. It was just the two of them in the world. Another whole day had passed, and still I was no nearer him than this. I went blind for a moment. When I could see again, I saw who Margo was. She was the enemy.

CHAPTER 4

THE NEXT DAY WAS CHRISTMAS EVE, THOUGH IT was hard to believe. The decorations we'd seen in Acapulco were plastic icicles curling in the sun. Here in this old bachelor's house there were no decorations at all. The red flowers in the pots around the pool were poinsettias, but there was nothing else. I was up so early that Luna hadn't found my room yet, and the house seemed asleep. I was up, wrenching myself out of bed, to find Dad.

The breakfast was laid out on a terrace that faced south across the bay, looking over to the opposite headland. Breakfast was there, under silver covers, for whoever wanted it, and only one person was here this early. Margo was here in shorts and a tube top for the sun on her shoulders and legs. It was too late to retreat, though I hung there at the edge of the terrace. I wasn't used to thinking of grown women as beautiful. To me, girls like Brooke were beautiful—like sleek colts with angular grace, leggy and burnished. The girls I wanted to be, nobody older.

Margo smiled and gestured to another chair, and I had to take it. A year younger, and I'd have turned my back and stalked away, but it was too late for that now. "Hot chocolate?" she said, and when she handed it to me in the mug, I knew who she reminded me of.

We hadn't talked, and now we had to. "When Brooke came to live with me, she must have been about the age you are now. Fifteen?"

"Fourteen," I said, "in five days."

She registered that with a slight lift of the eyebrow, the way Brooke would. She went on weaving her words, and I wondered if they were a net. "I'll miss Brooke next year when she's away at Middlebury. She's become a daughter to me in ways I hadn't expected. But she'll be in New York for holidays. You must come out, Jessica, and visit then."

My mind leaped off its leash at that—at the thought of going to New York and being in Brooke's world, of seeing her room. They lived on Park Avenue. I imagined going shopping and standing in one of

those three-way mirrors in a try-on room and seeing
Brooke and me there together.

But it wasn't quite an invitation, and I could see
how persuasive Margo could be. I could imagine her
selling expensive things to rich, uncertain people. The
aquamarine on her elegant hand drew the sunlight,
and her eyes were safe behind sunglasses. The cocoa
cooled in the mug in my hand.

Dad appeared, up from steps behind us that I
hadn't noticed. He'd been in the pool. A white towel
hung around his neck, and his trunks clung to him.
The dark hair was matted and glistening on his chest.
He looked first at Margo, and then noticed me.

"I never saw you up this early, sweetheart," he
said, and I could have said the same of him. When he
leaned down to brush my forehead with a kiss, drop-
lets of pool water fell from his beaded mustache.
"And what have you got planned for today?" he
asked me, but his eyes were skidding toward Margo.

Brooke and Tony and I were going into town tonight, late, to a club. *The* club, in fact—Baby O's. It
was our idea of celebrating Christmas Eve, but it was
hours away, the whole day. Dad had settled in a chair
past Margo's. He reached for her hand and said, "I
thought you and I might—"

"Scott, why don't you spend the day with Jessica,"
she said, and it wasn't a question.

"We could all three do something," he said. "Go someplace."

"No, you two. After all, you and Jessica haven't been together for months. When was it that you came down here, the end of summer?"

I tried not to hear. It wasn't going to be the day I wanted if she planned it. And I hadn't known he'd been down here all these months. I'd thought he was someplace even farther away, on location, someplace where you couldn't mail letters. But at least he hadn't been in New York with her. "Jess?" he said.

"What."

"Is there something you'd like to do?" He was working the towel over his head, and the curls of his hair were tight and dark. He hadn't shaved this morning, and his chin was blue. He could make movies. He was too good to be—

". . . Into town," he was saying. "You haven't been to Quebrada yet, where the boys dive off the cliff. Everybody has to see that. It's the Acapulco thing. And what else? What do kids like to do? They've got a water slide at Pie de la Cuesta."

"She's too old for a water slide, Scott," Margo said.

"We could hit one of the markets then," he said, "do some shopping. Come to think of it, I don't have your Christmas present yet, honey."

"Why don't you make today Jessica's present?"

Margo said in her even tone. Turning to me she said, "Men never know what kind of presents women really want."

It was the most flattering and grown-up thing anybody had ever said to me. I couldn't get my ears closed fast enough. She was lying back in the chair, her legs gleaming, between us, but she was handing Dad over to me, for the day. "Why don't you two just spend the day quietly together?"

"We could all meet later for lunch," he said.

"The whole day," Margo said.

It became a plan then. The fishermen weren't going out today. They were mending their nets or doing whatever they do on dry land. We'd go out on the boat and hire them as crew. It would be our own private yacht. Blanca could pack us a lunch. Dad and me on our own yacht out in the aquamarine bay. Perfect, if Margo hadn't tried to ruin it by making it happen. I couldn't believe how much she was like my—

"And honey," Dad said to me, "don't wear that swimsuit you had on yesterday. It's a little too advanced. Wear shorts and a shirt, or something."

Margo laughed, just a handful of musical notes.

Dad brought his camera. I supposed he was never without it, but he didn't take any pictures of me, because he'd brought the wrong lens for that. Baltazar and Roberto were crew. Baltazar was grizzled and middle-aged and seemed to be Blanca's husband. Roberto was a little monkey of a man. They ran the engine to take us out into the bay, and then they hoisted the sails, and we drifted. But we were becalmed as the sun climbed. Baltazar and Roberto disappeared below into the narrow, fishy-smelling cabin, and we could hear the slap of cards on a table.

It wasn't a day for photography. We hung in heat haze, and the rocky shoreline became even more unreal. It was a day to lie up at the pointed bow, slathered in number forty-four suntan oil, and watch the mast point a finger at the empty sky. You could sleep here. The sun almost insisted, and the fish smell in the deck boards was a drug. I could sleep now better than I'd slept all night, waiting to be up early. You could lie here on the narrow deck and float somewhere between sky and sea, earth and heaven.

"I should have brought my fishing gear," Dad said later.

"I've missed you," I said to him. It was what *he* should have said to *me.* We were lying here, our beach towels overlapping, as in all my dreams of this moment. He propped himself up on an elbow.

"No, you're too busy for that. I forget how old you're getting to be. You've got school and friends, and you wouldn't have time for your old man anyway."

"I miss you," I said again.

"There'll be boys pretty soon," he answered, looking past me. "That swimsuit you had on yesterday—there'll be boys."

"I go to a girls' school."

"That school was never my idea," Dad said, and I never thought it was. She—my mother made those decisions, all of them wrong.

"Your mother," he said, and so we weren't safe from her even here. "Your mother's doing fine, isn't she?"

"Better than I am."

"Your mother will be all right. She's strong. She'll marry again, I expect, if she wants to."

I'd never thought of that. It was disgusting, somebody else trying to take Dad's place. "Was she unfaithful to you? Was that why you left her?"

His Adam's apple moved, maybe in surprise. Then he smiled me back to childhood. "Your mother's not the unfaithful type. But we were married too young. One day I looked up, and I was staring forty in the face."

"Not yet."

"Soon," he said, which didn't explain a thing. There were only three ages: *now, high school,* and *grown up.* All adults were the same age until they got like Lucius Pirie. And why was divorce a solution for Dad, but a problem for me?

We drifted. Then the question rose up in me from a place so deep that it came out as a whisper.

"Dad, was it me?"

"What?" he said. "What do you mean?"

I didn't know. It wasn't even anything I'd thought. "Did I have something to do with you leaving?"

"You?" He shook his head and didn't look at me. "No, you didn't have anything to do with it."

Where was the comfort in that? Why didn't he reach out? Just a touch would have helped.

Still we drifted, but not together. Finally, I asked him, "Do you want Brooke's aunt to give your photographs a New York show?"

He blinked as if a baby had asked something very intelligent, or maybe a parrot.

"I'd thought of it earlier," he said. "After all, Margo represents Uncle Lucius's work, and she's the best there is. But no, not now. A show needs a shape, and it'll be a long time before I have the right work pulled together for it, if ever." He grinned, boyish. "Anyway, it isn't art if you sell it, is it?"

I didn't know. Lucius Pirie seemed to think it wasn't art unless you did sell it. Pictures became real when people saw them and wanted them. Maybe

there were different rules for paintings and photography. How could I know? And there was that little
distracting slap of the waves against the hull.

"You could be famous," I told him. "Famouser
than Lucius Pirie."

"Famouser?" Dad said.

"More famous. Just as famous. Don't you want to
be?"

He thought, and then said, "Maybe someday.
Maybe when I'm grown up." But that was silly. He
was already grown up.

"Hey, you're not worried that I have to sell my
work or starve, are you?"

No, I hadn't thought about it.

"Because I don't want you worrying about that.
Money takes care of itself," Dad said. "I couldn't han-
dle that New York art scene anyway. There are sharks
in those waters. Margo's a lot tougher than I am."

Did that put tough Margo in her place? Did that
leave her without claims on Dad? Baltazar and Roberto came up from below, carrying silver trays,
slightly dented, with our lunches on them: sandwiches
and tostadas with melted cheese, a bottle of mineral
water for me, a bottle of Carta Blanca for Dad. They
were perfect servants, though they looked more like
banditos. There were crocheted edges on the napkins,
and we ate our lunch in the blazing sun.

Now we were limp with sun and food, stretched out again on the deck. "Will you stay on down here?" I asked.

"Well, the fishing's good, and it's always summer. Everything's falling apart, of course—the house, the whole country, Uncle Lucius. But I'll stay on a while."

"I'll stay with you."

He smiled a lazy smile at that. He was lying on his stomach with his fingers laced under his chin, and I couldn't get used to his mustache. "What about that expensive school of yours?"

"I'll go to school here."

"How's your Spanish?"

"How's yours?"

"Quien sabe?" Dad said.

He was lying with his long back exposed to the sun. I poured oil into my hand and reached over to work it into his shoulders and down his back.

His eyes were closed, but at my first touch he said, "No, don't do that."

He'd made it wrong—me touching him. Everything. So I was left with the oil leaking through my fingers, and Dad beside me out of reach.

I didn't sleep after that, and time passed. Baltazar and Roberto sat in the stern, drinking Dos Equis beer. We'd drifted near the opposite shore of the bay,

and someone called out Dad's name. The sound woke
him, and we saw a man standing at the end of a pier,
his hand waving us in through the shimmering air.

He seemed to be a friend of Dad's. Baltazar started
the engine, and we came into his pier. It was elaborate, glaring white with white ropes and polished
brass fittings and pots of Aztec lilies. I don't remember the man's name. Maybe I never heard. I don't
think I did. He was little and round in a terrible
Fiorucci shirt, with a belly hanging over his shorts and
a cap like a commodore's.

"Come up for a drink, Scotty, to celebrate the season," he said. We climbed up a long flight of white
stairs and then a marble gravel path between rows of
tall cypress trees. Then the house, all sheets of glass
window with the kind of curtains that look like they
move on motors.

He had a wife, or at least a woman was there, taller
than the little round man, with blinding blond hair
and too much jewelry. Too thin too. She was a stick
figure who smoked. The house was outrageous, with
crystal pendants hanging off everything and too much
furniture. It was a house trying not to be in Mexico.
Worst of all, there was a Christmas tree, an artificial
white one they'd brought down from the States, with
blue glass balls all alike that reflected the room and us

at least a hundred times. The pictures on the walls were all color-coordinated.

They said all kinds of embarrassing things to me, like how could Scotty have a daughter as old as I was, and how I must take after my mother because I was lots better looking than Dad. Stupid things. But they were friendly in a loud way.

"You should send your boys home," they said, meaning Baltazar and Roberto, who were grown men. "We'll run you back later in the Jag."

But Dad said, "They'll wait."

Everybody had drinks, and mine looked like orange juice but tasted like syrup. I was thirsty, but not this thirsty. "Don't worry about the ice," the woman said through her smoke. "We have it made from bottled water. We disinfect everything." The furniture was covered in plastic that stuck to the backs of my legs. It all made me feel young enough to nag Dad about leaving, but I couldn't.

Time dragged, and the man droned on and on about fish and cars and the prices of things. He wore leather thongs, and there was hair growing on his toes. I was sticking to everything, including the glass. The woman said, "Maybe you'd like to wash up."

A skittery little maid in flip-flop sandals showed me to a bathroom down a mirrored hall. There were mirrors everywhere, and the bathroom was all black marble and purple towels. When I came out, I nearly walked into a mirror that reflected another room, a bedroom or a study. I looked in.

There in that room I saw something that shouldn't have been there. I could have walked across and reached out and . . .

I didn't know where I was for a moment. I closed my eyes against—the room and everything, and didn't open them again until I was walking away down the hall, hurrying, following the voices that came from the big room with the disgusting tree. The disgusting fake tree in this disgusting house where everything was fake, except for one thing. And I shouldn't have seen it.

When we left, Baltazar and Roberto were waiting down in the boat to ferry us back across the bay. On our own pier Dad reached into his shorts pocket and pulled out a big roll of American money and peeled off some bills for Baltazar and Roberto, who took them.

Brooke and Tony and I went out that night to Baby O's. It was the place to be in Acapulco that winter. I'd thought I didn't want to go, even though I had something new to wear. I couldn't think of any place I wanted to be that evening. But I'd have followed Brooke and Tony anywhere—to the moon. The nighttime city gleamed around a bay full of cruise ships outlined in white light.

Baby O's was like Paradise after dark: thousands of people and more of them jockeying to get in. But doors had a way of opening for Tony. It had to do with his blond hair and big arms and that open face that made you think the good times were wherever he was. He found us a table and a pitcher of Dos Equis. I drank some, but Brooke kept an eye on me. It was a big mall of a room done like a jungle cavern with climbing vines and strobe lights.

I hadn't done much dancing before, only what our group did at Rhonda's house, bopping around her bedroom and falling over the furniture. Rhonda always chose the tapes. Tony got me out on the floor a couple of times, and it wasn't much like Rhonda's room. Glitter dropped through strobe light beams, and they had a smoke machine. The floor was glass brick with revolving colors beneath.

It was crazy music: La Cucaracha meets Mötley Crüe, and everything had that Acapulco heat and beat. I was scared, but Tony was good. He didn't let me fall down or disappear into the crowds. The best part was watching him dance with Brooke. They moved together, even apart. Every time she turned back to him, he was there.

I'd bought a black cotton top with a wide mouth

that pulled off one shoulder. And the shortest skirt I'd had since third grade. Brooke loaned me a woven Mexican sash in all colors to knot around my waist and one hip. I'd wondered about makeup, but she said it would look like I was trying too hard. She said it was okay to be the age I was. She tied back my hair the way she wore hers during the day, and it gave me cheekbones.

Baby O's was a forgetful kind of place. You couldn't think and you couldn't talk, and time didn't count. The music did it all for you.

We came home late, but Acapulco never really sleeps. People sat out along the Costera, playing cards at tables under the street lights. When we made that sweeping turn around the headland, it was black sea ahead, all the way to China.

At home, Luna and the other dogs were loose in the grounds. Their eyes burned in the headlights, but they didn't raise the alarm. Tony said they knew the sound of his car, and they could tell we weren't strangers anyway. They were very intelligent, he said, all magna cum laude. We had to stumble around to find the back gate that led to Tony's *caseta.* It was at the end of the kitchen garden, perfumed by the creosote bushes. His place was just a shape at the end, a little thick-walled hut that had been there before the house. By then, everything struck us as funny, and it was a great achievement not to trip over things and fall.

At some point Lucius Pirie had fixed up the place as a guest cottage and strung a wire out here for lights. The ceiling looked like tree branches. Tony had a bed and an oil lamp for when the electricity failed. He worked at a sawhorse table with a laptop word processor and a small library of art books. Lucius Pirie had let him bring paintings down from the house to study. They were propped around like a studio.

One big picture stood on an easel. Its colors were true enough to bring daylight in. Lucius Pirie had painted it from the terrace, looking out to sea. Both of the long points of land that make the bay were there, and the shoreline rocks rose out of the surf like the beginning of time. It was this place as it had always been, before people, as if nothing human could hurt it.

"He was at the peak of his powers then," Tony said. "His technique and that other indefinable quality were working together then."

"What a wonderful thing to live with," Brooke said.

Tony nodded. "I keep it here to see when I wake up."

Borrowing their eyes, I saw this picture as if I'd never seen one before. Even in this light it was its own world. Lucius Pirie was a great artist. This picture proved it, and the others were echoes.

"It's funny," Tony said. "His Mexican work is his critical success, and yet he was best known earlier for his portraits of society women. In his youth he was called 'the new Sargent.' "

I didn't know who John Singer Sargent was and didn't find out till afterwards, in an art appreciation course during junior year. But I thought of the portrait Lucius Pirie had done of my grandmother Ferris, though I'd been trying to forget it. The unfinished portrait of Jessica.

Back in the big house, Brooke and I found our way in the dark, and finally we were in the hall that led past her bedroom and ended with mine. She followed me to see that I really got there. I knew where the light switch was, but a wonderful soft breeze was coming in from the sea. Brooke and I went outside on the little porch, for the night air on our faces.

From there we could look down to the swimming-pool terrace. The pool was lighted from beneath, a long rectangle more aquamarine than the daytime sea, set in darkness. Brooke made a little sound beside me.

There was no other sound, unless I'd gone deaf. Two people were in the pool. Not swimming. They were embracing, locked together. She had one hand on the edge of the pool, and the other around his shoulders. His hand was in her hair. Their clothes were scattered on the terrace where they'd dropped them, and the bright water moved around them. Margo and Dad.

CHAPTER 5

CHRISTMAS DAY, WITH SOME KIND OF PARTY later in the cool of the evening, if the day ever ended.

I'd slept as long as I could, until the noontime heat brought me to the surface. I'd had a dream, that I was out on the water again, but alone in a boat dragging its anchor across an empty bay. Dad wasn't there at all. Apparently I'd sailed in this boat all the way from Chicago, over mountains and across deserts to be here, but I was drifting alone.

I woke up lying in a shape of my own sweat, head pounding with the same anger I'd taken to bed. Luna was asleep on the floor, splayed out like a trophy, to feel the cool tiles, dead to the world.

I'd come all this way so I wouldn't have to live

holed up in my room back home, and now I was going to have to live holed up in this one. There was nowhere else for me to be. I'd come here on a fool's errand.

A maid came in to make the bed and found me in it. Nobody wanted me, but I had no privacy. The lock on the door didn't work, and there was that gaping space that looked outdoors, and down to that terrible view of the pool. I hadn't seen her before, but she was a maid because her look went straight to the floor, where I'd thrown my clothes and the bright sash that Brooke had loaned me.

She was only a child, younger than I was, working for her living. She was no more than ten, barefoot, in a smock, with her hair in a long pigtail. It made her look like a miniature woman. Her eyes were huge, waiting for her face to grow up.

I climbed out of bed without saying anything to her, because I didn't have anything to say to anybody. As long as she was in the room, I wouldn't get dressed, so I stood, cornered. She made my bed, and her arms were like a sparrow's, if sparrows had arms. Then she was gone.

Even she had looked like a woman, a tiny one. The world was full of women who set traps for my dad. When he was free of one, another snared him. The world was made up of women like my mother who held him with their powers. They had this network of nets. But I had rights to him nobody else had. I was his flesh and blood, and these women had robbed me.

It was hard to breathe. The loops of mosquito netting were motionless, and there wasn't a fly-buzz of sound. Not a boat in the bay. Where were they now? Dad and—her. I didn't even know where his room was, and I didn't want to, because maybe they . . . shared.

I wasn't going to have anything more to do with her. I wasn't even going to be in the same room with her, or at the same table. Then it occurred to me what I was going to do.

Taking clothes into the bathroom, I gave myself a birdbath at the sink and did what I could with my hair. When I ran water to splash on my face, it came out of the faucet in fits and starts, and slightly brown. *Never drink the water.* Even my mother had warned me. I cupped my hands and drank a handful of water and then three more, swallowing fast in case it tasted. I drank straight out of the faucet. There was a bottle of safe water for brushing your teeth. Crazily, I used it to brush mine.

I went back to my room and waited to be sick. When I was little, it was my mother who'd sat next to my bed. My mother had put the cold washcloths on my forehead and had taken my temperature and had held the basin. I rewrote this history to put my dad there in her place. To hurry things up, I imagined the bacteria or whatever darting like dragonflies across surfaces in my stomach. I felt bloated, which was a start, and soon I'd be doubled up. Dad would be here beside me through the days and nights. Dad—worried, frantic—would be here with me and nowhere else.

I lay stretched out on the bed waiting, but time wouldn't pass. To help it along, I reached for _Love's Incandescence._ I read furiously, the way I'd slept. Back to the Scottish heroine of clan MacLaren who was willing to sacrifice everything, even her life, for her dark lover.

She reminded me of Brooke, though I didn't want her to. Brooke had been startled at the sight of Margo and Dad in the pool with nothing between them. Startled, but not surprised. She'd known about them and hadn't told me. Rhonda would have. Rhonda would have come running. Rhonda would have told me at the airport.

But not Brooke. She'd known they were—lovers, and so she was part of the plot. She stood too near the world of adults to be trusted.

I'd hoped that Margo was this businesswoman Dad needed to be nice to because of business. I thought he was being nice to her so she'd give his photography a

show in her bigtime New York gallery. I'd believed
that as long as I could. Now I couldn't trust that the-
ory anymore. Could I trust Brooke? Maybe she was
just another Margo. Maybe she and Tony—

Then her shadow fell across the floor. The sun had
finally moved from the dead center of the sky, so she
threw a shadow when she came in from the porch. I
thought of not looking up from my book, but I already had. I put a finger with a ragged nail on a word
I chose at random.

"We checked on you earlier, and you were practically in a coma," she said. "Tony and I." Over her
swimsuit she wore a white shirt, maybe Tony's.

I didn't know whether to sulk or not. Was she
friend or enemy? But it didn't matter. Pretty soon
now I was going to be spectacularly sick. I wouldn't
want her in the room then—just Dad. She could wait
out in the hall. I turned down the corner of the page
and sat up to hear her plans for the evening and what
we were going to wear. At the mall of the Condesa
we'd bought wild Mexican dresses, very ethnic, for
the occasion. But I wouldn't have the occasion to be
wearing mine. So I made my eyes round and unsulky
while she talked.

Her sunglasses were on top of her head, and she
stood with one lovely hand around the bedpost, and
you could see the suggestion of her figure through

the white shirt. Though I wasn't sure who she was now, I still wanted to be her. But I was too solemn or something. She was watching me.

"You feel okay?"

I said I felt all right because I did, so far.

"I slept a lot at your age too," she said, measuring the years between us. She'd run out of conversation, and I didn't have any more for her. Her hand dropped off the bedpost. "Jessica, you're not upset about—anything?"

I referred that to my stomach and shook my head.

At the door she turned back. Lingering, she watched me, and there were a couple of little sympathy lines in her forehead. "Listen, don't worry," she said. "It's all right, really. Don't . . . overreact." Then she went away.

Somehow I couldn't get sick, and finally Brooke came back for me. I had to put on my fiesta dress, or maybe I wanted to. I'd chosen a dress as like hers as I'd dared. They were simple, loose cotton that fell straight from the shoulder to the floor, embroidered in flowers of all clashing colors. The kind of thing you wear in Mexico and then hang in the back of the closet at home for the rest of your life. Brooke cinched hers at the waist with a silver-link belt.

In the kitchen, where we went to see the preparations, Blanca was overseeing three or four women. One kneaded the corn dough, the masa, for tortillas. They weren't in any hurry, going about their work without an unnecessary gesture. The only familiar thing was the smell of a turkey roasting in the big institutional oven. Now I was hungry, which was embarrassing. When we were leaving the big dim room, I noticed the children clustered in corners and looking out from under worktables with big eyes, waiting for Christmas to begin.

The party was to be indoors, in the living room because it cooled first. I'd only looked in there before. It opened in a grand sweep across the far end to a high view of the sea and the steps to the swimming pool. The beams in the ceiling were heavy and painted and touched with gilt. The furniture was Spanish. Lucius Pirie's work hung on the walls: landscapes and portraits. Women out of the past who were too pale for this country, swanlike women in gowns that fell from their milk-white shoulders, and Mexican women, too, in earth tones, with faces like woodcarvings.

It was almost a museum, and Lucius Pirie was there at the center of the room like the most ancient work of art. Enthroned in a chair, he sat all in white under a wide-brimmed Panama hat. Behind him stood the man who served him and no one else. He was in white, too, as always. His name was Martin, and his smooth dark face was shaped like a shield. Lucius Pirie sat on his throne, recovering from his siesta, he said. Dad and Tony were there. And Margo. I was in the same room with her, though I'd promised myself not to be. But I had no power.

She sat in a low sofa with her legs crossed at the knee. Her dress was black, with lush white silk flowers across the neck and shoulders. I wouldn't look at her face, now that I knew every woman's face was my mother's.

Instead I watched Dad there in the glow of the paintings, listening to Tony's impassioned talk about them. The child in me darted forward, dodging furniture to circle my dad like a vine the way small children can, to stand on his feet and pull at his fingers separately, to pry attention with an upflung face, wielding the rights of childhood.

But I'd lost even the power of a child and stood rooted, far from him still, in a dress Rhonda wouldn't have approved. *When I'm grown,* I said almost aloud, but the future was a blank, even if I hadn't taken a lethal dose of tap water. At fourteen you think you've already waited as long as you can. And I wasn't even fourteen yet.

The party began. It was for the children of Lucius Pirie's people. Invisible hands urged them into the room. The first was a brave little boy scrubbed to a high sheen, who tried to turn back and then led the others. His eyes wondered at the room, and he closed them tight when he caught sight of Lucius Pirie looming there in that scary hat. But he kept walking. After him came little girls like toy bridesmaids in stiffened peach skirts and polished white shoes and frilly socks. They were terrified and tempted, and I remembered Santa Claus on his throne at Marshall Field's. The older children followed, carrying the babies and leading the ones who were only beginning to walk. They moved with the grace of their parents, with the grace of this country, where people carry themselves with patient pride.

The boy in the lead never faltered. He presented himself to the great man. Thinking he might be too small to be noticed, he reached up and touched the enormous old hand. Martin conjured up presents from behind the throne, and Lucius Pirie handed them over. Toys for everybody and dolls for the little girls, wonderful things all in big explosions of cellophane. They were stunned by this magnificence. At the end of the line of children was the girl who'd made my bed, in her smock, still on duty. The grownups came behind her, all but Blanca and the women working in the kitchen. The gardeners came in, hats in hands, and Roberto, the little man from the boat.

"Feliz Navidad," Lucius Pirie said to them in his cracked voice. He shook their hands, closed their hands in both of his, and something passed between them.

At the end of the line, Lucius Pirie looked up for Baltazar, grizzled but in a clean shirt, weaving toward him like the floor was a deck. Lucius Pirie put out his arms, and Baltazar leaned down to embrace him, to give him the *abrazo.* So they were old friends, old campaigners, and who knew if this was the last Christmas that would find them both in this room? Now it *felt* like Christmas.

There was a piñata and sacks of candy for the children, and rounds of presents for us all: wine and perfume and piñata trinkets. Christmas was shining in the children's eyes. I should have slipped away then, back to my room.

The six of us had our Christmas dinner in the courtyard at the heart of the house. It was the moment before dark, and you could see the yucca in flower with long arcs of blossom like waxen, cream-colored bells. The blossoms fell, drifting like snow across the table and mingling with the white poinsettia between the candles.

I sat in the place where Margo had sat on the first night, next to Dad. She altered course and went to sit on Lucius Pirie's right, where I had been. She moved with more grace than I did, but I was next to Dad now. And Lucius Pirie was glad to see her there. His hand with the enormous turquoise ring moved to cover hers, and I placed my hand on the table, too, in case Dad wanted to cover mine. I was there between him and Tony. What better place? Sunstruck Tony, with his peeling nose and a sprig of plastic holly out of the piñata in the pocket of his shirt. And Dad like a bronze of himself in the warm, flickering candlelight.

Blanca brought in the turkey on a huge platter. There was cranberry sauce, straight out of the can and sliced into moons. But everything else was Mexican: mild-looking pastries that weren't, chilies in everything, and *queso fundido,* a cheese sauce that would take off the roof of your mouth. I ate now, deciding to forget I was sending this feast down into a stomach as polluted as the bay at Acapulco.

We had paper hats to wear in that screaming watermelon-pink of Mexico. I forget what mine was, but Brooke's was a crown, and Tony's had Mouseketeer ears. Dad's was a pirate's hat, which was about right with the deep tan that made his teeth whiter than white.

He'd shaved off his mustache. When I saw, he shrugged. "I had the idea you liked the clean-shaven look better."

It was Christmas now—better, with Dad not an

arm's length away and Tony on the other side. The white flowers fell across the table, gusted by conversation. Lucius Pirie dozed lightly between the courses and sometimes during. He kept on his big grandee's straw hat, maybe to keep from wearing a paper one, and the brim dipped as he slipped in and out of sleep. We even sang carols: "Good King Wenceslas," for the fun of the line about the snow lying round about, deep and crisp and even. Then at the end there was flan again, because a plum pudding would be too heavy. Lucius Pirie called for Blanca and the other women from the kitchen, and Baltazar again. He came in bearing a tray with a special pineapple wine in thimble glasses. Blanca drank a glass, too, somber as church, though a smile had escaped her when she raised her glass to our host.

We sat back from the table, and I pulled my chair nearer Dad's. His hand was on my shoulder, and in his other was the wine glass with the swallow of yellow nectar sparked by candlelight. The world narrowed to this perfect courtyard and then burst like a bubble.

I looked along the table to where Brooke's and Margo's profiles almost matched. The white silk flowers caressed the dark shoulders of Margo's dress. She didn't wear a paper hat. Her hair was drawn back and up tonight, held there with a comb or something that glittered.

Something else glittered, apart from the comb and her smile. Her ears were alight with diamonds. Now I was staring. She wore diamond earrings, and when she turned this way to glance at Dad, I saw that they were the distinctive earrings that had been my mother's, and before her, Grandmother Ferris's in her portrait by Lucius Pirie.

The courtyard shaded to red, and something sharp turned in my brain. The napkin fell off my lap onto the ground because now I was standing up. People looked at me, and the conversation stopped. I hadn't said anything much all evening. Being between Tony and Dad had been enough.

Because he'd given Margo the earrings, I pointed at her. "You're a thief," I said loud. "You stole those earrings. You steal things."

I turned and fell over the chair and ran without looking. Time slowed as I lurched and swerved, running from the room. Behind me, jolted from a dream, Lucius Pirie said, "Who is that child?"

CHAPTER 6

THEN I WAS SOMEWHERE ELSE. SOME "NO PLACE," where I was alone. I'd wanted to lash out at Margo, to show them what she was, to show Dad. But now they'd all hate me, and I wasn't used to being blamed for anything. I was used to blaming. Tony came to find me after what felt like hours. I must have been in my room. I was in a corner somewhere at the end of the world.

"Hey, you really know how to break up a party."

"Don't," I said, but of them all, he was the one I was least afraid of. He stood with his big arms folded across his chest, hang-loose as ever.

"Look, we'll all live," he said. "I was embarrassed once myself."

"When?"

I think he grinned. "That was a joke. Everybody gets embarrassed all the time. Especially guys."

"Nothing is worse for guys," I said to the only guy I knew. He let that pass, and so I said, "Where are they?"

"Who?"

"Them."

"Well, it's past Lucius Pirie's bedtime," Tony said.

"He doesn't even know who I am," I said, sulky. " 'Who is that child?' he said."

"He knows," Tony said, "but you woke him up. When he's dreaming, he goes back in time."

I wished I could.

"Brooke's called it a day. She's in her room giving herself a pedicure or doing whatever girls do when they retire to the repair shop." Tony stood at the edge of my space in a correctly faded Hawaiian shirt. Now his hands were propped in his pants pockets—tux pants with a stripe, with red high-top Converses. Festive.

"And Scott—your dad—and Margo have gone for a drive in the station wagon."

I burned at that.

"Hey, that's how it works," Tony said. "You attack Margo, and your dad makes it up to her."

That wasn't the way it should work. I had a perfect

right to say anything I felt like to women who reminded me of my mother. I hated Tony for a second, before he said, "You haven't been crying, have you?"

Not yet. The red splotches on my face were temper, and that other thing you feel when it's too late to turn back.

"You look like you're tied up in a tight knot and can't find the loose end."

I _was_ in a tight knot, including my stomach.

"Want to go out?" he said.

"Where?"

"Anyplace. The night's young. It's hardly dawn."

"But where?" I was unknotting. Tony didn't hate me.

"I don't know. You name it."

"A beach," I said, "a real one you can walk on."

It's what I'd wanted before I came to this place: a long, empty beach with nobody else around, the kind that didn't seem to exist here. I'd dreamed of Dad and me walking a deserted beach with the cool of the surf between our toes as it scalloped the sand. I rewrote the dream and put Tony in Dad's place. When I dared look up at him, he was holding out his arms.

We took a flashlight and followed a path I hadn't noticed. It was downhill with drops to the rocks on one side. As we climbed down, the cliffs began to tower over us. The flashlight created the path. It would have been scary if I hadn't wanted to get away from the house. It was jungly and spikey and surely a mile.

We came to a hidden place somewhere along the lip of the bay. It was a long half-moon of sand, not the endless beach of my dreams. Maybe better, more mysterious. There's nothing as mysterious as Mexico after dark. It's as black and vivid as those paintings on velvet they sell along the road. We kicked off our shoes to leave them where we could find them again. Now we were trudging through the sand, with Tony's arm casually around my shoulder.

It was brighter somehow, after the path. A bar of green glowed along the sea horizon, and the sand was salted by starlight. Tony's arm was still around me. He was cooling me off in the close, warm night. At night, Mexico smells like musky perfume.

At the far end was a rock he knew about, almost an island. We waded the last steps. It was sea-smoothed and dry. Sitting on it, we were almost out in the bay among the odd lights in the water. Tropical sea creatures sent out bluish impulses.

I'd have settled for silence, but finally Tony said, "You'll have to meet my dad some day."

I hadn't thought about him having a dad.

"He's a kidder," Tony said. "A big guy, too, a big, round guy. I'm going to have to keep working out so

I don't get like that. He's the kind of guy who does card tricks at parties. He goes to the gag-and-magic shop at the mall and stocks up on stuff to entertain people: rubber chickens, dribble glasses, whoopee cushions. He's the life of the party."

He sounded awful, embarrassing. "What's your mother like?"

"Patient," Tony said. "Understanding. She knows he really needs the world to love him. She knows he has to keep trying."

Time passed, and we listened. The sea made overlapping sounds. Wings whispered from the trees.

"You kind of came at Margo from the wrong direction," he said after a while. "The earring thing. Your dad had given the earrings to her, I guess as a Christmas present. She didn't want them, and she didn't know their history. She isn't the type to take jewelry from men. She can buy her own jewelry. She'd only worn them tonight to please him. You got to her, though, if she was the one you were gunning for."

Who else would I be gunning for? But I'd have turned back the clock if I could.

I wanted to hate Margo, but she was too . . . elusive. Here in the dark I couldn't even picture her face. And I couldn't blame Dad. It was my oldest rule.

"It isn't fair," I said, and Tony let that pass too.

"On the other hand," he said after a little while, "in a year or two, you'll—"

"How did you like it," I asked him, "when people used to say you'd grow out of things?"

"Nobody ever thought I would," he said.

"My dad says when I start knowing guys, I'll forget all about him. I won't. How could I? And what about now? At my age all you can do is watch other people living. Then when you open your mouth, garbage comes out."

"That's good," Tony said. "I mean it's good that you can explain it."

"It doesn't help. I bet you can't even remember being my age, because there's nothing to remember."

He thought about that. Then he said, "I seem to remember sleeping with my skateboard and wondering if I was a dwarf. You're right. It's not great. How old would you choose to be if you could just change, right now?"

That was a weird question because my mind split in two. One of me went back to being little. I didn't go back to that winter day in the park with Dad, but I went back that far. I caught a glimpse of me on a beach, the Oak Street Beach across the Drive from our apartment. My mother had taken me through the underpass, with the traffic whizzing over our heads and rumbling the tunnel. Then we came out on the beach, and it was summer in Chicago, the season you wait for. The beach was full of people, and there were nets set up for volleyball. We'd brought a blanket, and I had a little shovel and a pail for making sand castles. The sand was warm and ran through my fingers. I played there just next to the blanket where my mother sat.

But another of my selves went in the other direction. What age would I want to be if I could be any? Brooke's, of course. Brooke, who moved in the direction of the world and was already there.

"Brooke," I said.

"Ah, yes," Tony answered, "the lovely Brooke."

Why that did it I don't know, but I was crying now. Tony was only humoring me like a child. But now he lifted my chin with a finger, and I was turning up a blotchy-feeling face in the luminous night. He kissed me. It was my first, but he knew how. I forgot to put my arms around him, and my hands were in a heap in my lap. I wasn't even sure I was ready for this, which is another drawback of a girls' school.

I didn't even know if it counted. It was only a comfort kiss, and now he was giving my shoulder a squeeze, which was a little too brotherly. Still, I felt better for another five minutes or so. Then the rock seemed unsteady beneath us, and the sea was suddenly too bright, too noisy. I saw colors in my head before the big bang, and then I was sick, spectacularly sick all over the rock. Gagging, retching sick on my knees with Tony holding my head. I was turning inside out and so was the world, and still I was stupendously sick.

And Tony was saying, "Hey, it was just a kiss."

CHAPTER 7

I WAS JUST AS SICK AS I'D PLANNED TO BE AND
then some. You have to be pretty careful about your
intake in Mexico. There was a day I don't remember
and another I'd just as soon forget. But it wasn't how
I thought it would be. Someone sat with me most of
the time. Silent Blanca would sometimes be there
very late. Never Dad.

Through half-open eyes I saw him once at the door.
I still had the basin in the bed with me, and though he
looked in on me, he didn't look at me. I lay still and
tried to appear as pathetic as possible because I didn't
know how mad he might be. But I remembered that
he never liked the sickroom. He was never there

through all the ills, real and not so real, that had kept me home from school. He went away then, as usual.

On the third day when I woke up early, there was a tray of tea and dry toast by the bed. Margo was sitting there. I wasn't ready for this. I must have thought I'd already been punished enough.

She was wearing a long-sleeved white silk blouse, not right for this climate, but then she never sweated. And a tweedy skirt that looked out of place too. Her hair was swept back efficiently, and her tan was perfect, even around the ears. Her earrings were black onyx in Mexican silver. "Better?" she said.

"Some, I think."

"It happens down here, even when you're careful."

She reached across and put her palm on my forehead to see if I still had a temperature. Her hand was cool, and I didn't pull away.

"You're on the road to recovery," she said. "On my first visit to Mexico, I ate a large and lethal green salad and thought I'd never see the end of it."

I couldn't imagine her bent double over a basin, or a rock, being unglamorously sick. At that moment I couldn't really imagine her in my father's arms either.

"Look on the bright side," she was saying. "Think of all the immunities you're developing." We sat almost looking at each other. I'd edged up in the bed, and I tried to remember what I had against her.

"You were so sick that first night," she said, shaking her head at the memory. I didn't remember. I couldn't seem to recall her hovering over me, but she must have been there. "Brooke and I took you in turns for most of the next day. You finally settled down and slept out of pure exhaustion. Still, you weren't over it."

No, yesterday I'd had a few more episodes, dry ones.

"I hoped you'd be better before I left. I'm going today."

It explained the clothes she wore, the matching tweed jacket hanging from the back of her chair. She was leaving, and I wondered if—

"Oh, no, don't worry." She put up a beautifully manicured hand. "Brooke's staying on. She doesn't need to be back at once, but I should. The holidays are really the only time of the year when you can get paperwork done. And after the first of the year I'm running over to London. There's an auction at Christie's. Nineteenth-century watercolors, and the word is that they'll go for less than they're worth."

She reached down and picked up something to hand over to me, a present tied in a bow. A slender book, it seemed to be. "The gallery had these printed several years ago, and I thought you might like to have a copy. A birthday present."

My birthday was tomorrow, if I hadn't lost track of time, but tomorrow she'd be gone. It crossed my mind to wonder if she'd reminded Dad that my birthday was coming. My mother always had to. It was hard to remember, coming so soon after Christmas.

The book was a catalogue with color prints, called *Lucius Pirie's Mexico,* and the cover illustration was a fine, faintly impressionist work of the fishing boats against the arching rocks at Cabo San Lucas. "Los Arcos," the painting was called. It was a grown-up kind of present, a keepsake. "Thank you," I said.

She was gathering herself to go. She moved like some sleek animal, a gazelle or something. With a glance at her watch she said, "My plane leaves at noon. Hard to believe it's winter in New York and the snow will be 'lying round about, deep and crisp and even.' "

Then I blurted out the question. "Is Dad going with you?"

"Oh, Jessica, no. Nothing like that." She stood by the bed, beautiful, lingering a moment. "It was just a vacation, you see. It was just for these few days. We all need a little unreality once in a while."

She'd gathered up her purse and opened it. "Of all things to forget," she said, digging around. She held the diamond earrings out to me.

"Here, keep these in the family." She could have

dropped them in a glittery pile on the table by the bed, but she held them out to me. When I took them, our hands touched.

"I'm sorry about what I said to you. What I called you."

"Oh, my dear," she said, "if 'thief' is the worst thing you ever call another woman, you'll be a candidate for sainthood."

At the door she said, "Good-bye, Jessica. Be well and happy."

I never saw her again because I never went to visit Brooke in New York, never saw her Park Avenue room or her life. Margo left me there on the road to recovery. Whether I'd driven her away or whether that was merely the day she planned to go, I didn't know. Even if I'd dared to ask, I couldn't have learned from Brooke, who was as smooth as her aunt. I wouldn't have asked. I wouldn't have risked Brooke's anger. But if I'd driven Margo away, it didn't feel as good as I'd have thought.

Dad didn't turn on me for insulting his—for insulting Margo. If he reacted at all, it was in turning away. Dad went off for a fishing trip up the coast toward Zihuatanejo with Baltazar and Roberto as crew. A difficult child spoiling a party could only speed him on his way.

I got over being sick. Pretty soon it was the three of

us again, Tony and Brooke and I, tearing up the roads in his neon-pink car, in our headgear. Thanks to my illness, I hadn't overdone the sun, and I emerged from the sickbed with my tan intact. Better, I had a waist now. Though I'd lost weight the hard way, I'd lost a lot. Brooke and I were now very roughly the same dimensions, if I could just grow a little more in a couple of directions.

Humoring me, maybe, Tony often put me in the front seat and Brooke went in the back. We drove around the Costera to see the divers at Quebrada. It's one of those things everybody does in Acapulco.

There's an old hotel, the Mirador, with terraces cut into the cliffs. From the highest one, the bronzed and glistening boys dive. After they've swarmed up the steep path, they kneel at an altar in a little blue and yellow shrine and pray for their lives.

Then a boy in Speedo trunks poises himself at the top outcropping of rock. Even from here you can see his toes curl like talons around the sharp stone. He looks down, reading the foamy, polluted sea where it gushes in through a cleft in the cliffs. Just at that moment before the water is deep enough he arches his back and throws his arms wide and dives.

It's close to flying, and there's a second when he's suspended motionless, brown, with blue sky behind him. Then he drops with supernatural control into that narrow, rushing channel of the sea. He's in the air a long time. It's a hundred and thirty feet, long enough for all the bus-tour people to click their cameras. It's a sight you have to see in Acapulco: boys trained from birth to risk their lives for the tips of tourists.

After the show the divers stand in a row on the tile of the terrace, and their bodies are miraculous up close, taut and sleek, because after all, they're sea creatures. They stand in puddles of saltwater, accepting the dollar bills that grow damp in their hands.

In the evenings we would drive in to sit at a table outside a café called the Flor de Acapulco in the old town square, the *zocalo*. This was the heart of the old city, all the way around the bay from the hotel strip, the only really authentic part. "Mexico at last," Tony called it. The sea was on one side and the white, Moorish-looking cathedral on the other. It was always crowded with people and worked by the soft-drink vendors and the shoeshine boys. But there was something villagy, rural about it. It was overgrown with trees that brought on evening earlier, and they had concerts in the bandstand.

Brooke and Tony ate, and I sipped the closest thing to a 7-Up I could find. It was the best place we went. "And the most foreign," Brooke said, "more exotic, more alien than Europe."

I didn't know. I'd only been to London, when my mother took me there. She had some kind of business to take care of. I was only seven or eight, and we didn't stay long. About all I remembered were red buses and Big Ben. Mexico was a lot more exotic than that.

When we weren't being tourists, we lounged around on the pier after the heat of the day, watching the sun climb down into the Pacific. It gave Tony a chance to wear a knotted red bandanna around his head, street-gang style. Somehow we never used the pool, or hung out on the swimming-pool terrace.

One evening as the sun was divided by the horizon, a fishing boat drew into our pier, a hired boat with some sports-fishing types down from the States. They were three or four men, middle-aged, in shorts and canvas hats. They'd come in to show us their catch.

Then we were all three looking down into the boat. They had this long pole with a steel hook on the end of it, and they were holding up what they'd taken out of the sea. It was a snake, the biggest snake I'd ever seen. They'd killed it, but it was still wet and iridescent from the water. White underneath and thick in the body beyond your worst nightmare of snakes, it stretched from one end of the boat to the other, and it was still moving, undulating like the sea. But it was dead. One of the sportsmen had hooked it up just below the spade-shaped head.

There was something beautiful about it, too, which made it worse. Only minutes ago it had been moving through the sea like a thick whiplash, its waterproof eyes watching, its fangs poised and poisonous. Brooke stepped back and pulled me back. She was rigid with the horror of it and of the men's pride in killing it. Tony was stunned, too, and I think it made him a little sick. The boat pulled away, and the engine shot smoke into the water. They propped the dead snake's head over the side where they wouldn't step on it, and they went away over the wavering water.

Shuddering, Brooke said almost in a whisper, "Nobody can really understand what this country means." Her face was gray, and I wouldn't have recognized her. I'd thought nothing could touch her. But there was death everywhere here, even the death of your dreams.

My dad came back from his fishing trip the next afternoon, browner and more boyish than before, gritty and unshaven and handsomer. I was thinner now. I could have worn Brooke's black Lycra swimsuit and gotten away with it.

"Look at you," Dad said that evening in the courtyard at dinner. So he must have noticed. My eyes were bigger in my face. And I was a year older, though he didn't remember, and nobody had reminded him. But I hadn't needed a birthday party with presents. I had a present, from Margo.

We were only four at the table because Lucius Pirie couldn't preside at a dinner table with guests every night. Margo was gone, and that may have taken the heart out of the party for him. Uncle Lucius said they were alike, that they both made long plans and nobody got in their way.

Dad sat at the head of the table, as the nephew of the house. Brooke sat at the other end with an hibiscus in her hair, and I was across from Tony, whose nose was still peeling.

Dad was like a kid about fishing, and about being out in a boat and away. He told us where they'd tied up for the night and the places they'd gone. It crossed my mind that for Dad it had been a vacation from a vacation, but for Baltazar and Roberto it had been a job. When Dad's arms came out to show us the size of an imaginary fish, his hand brushed mine.

There ought to be a time limit on fish stories, but his went on through all of Blanca's courses. He turned to me. "Jess, you should have been there." His hand closed over mine.

As if he'd have taken me with him, if I hadn't been sick. I was close to opening my hands and walking away and letting Dad walk away. I was close, but not close enough.

I still didn't have all my strength back. I was liable to doze off anywhere, even in Tony's car bucketing down the highway, and always on the pier. I went to my room early that night, and Tony went back to the *caseta* to catch up on his work.

Ready for bed, I stood in front of the tin-framed mirror and brushed out my hair in rhythmic strokes. I'd decided to let it grow below my shoulders, like Brooke's. Distant music played on the heavy air. It was often there in the background at night, wafting across the bay from some faraway house. Faint music with a Latin beat softened by sea breeze.

It drew me out onto my porch, the hairbrush still in my hand. The moon seeped through clouds, touching the sea with silver. I looked out on the night as if I might be saying good-bye.

Below, the swimming pool glowed like an aquamarine. Brooke was on the terrace by the low wall, so quiet that I hadn't seen her at first. She was looking toward the sea. We hadn't dressed up for dinner tonight. She was wearing a cotton top and a breezy skirt with a scarf tied around her waist, her usual elegance. I remembered the hibiscus in her hair, though I couldn't see it from here.

Dad came down the steps from the house. His shirt

and pants glowed, and he was barefoot, moving without sound. He circled the pool to where Brooke was. She turned suddenly when she realized he was there, but even in surprise her movements flowed like Margo's.

I couldn't hear what they said. She put her head back, perhaps smiling. He stretched out his arms, embracing the night. He used the music in the background, inviting her to dance, and she laughed. I heard a little peal of that, a handful of musical notes. They began to move, regular slow dancing that didn't match the music. The underwater light from the pool swayed over them. They turned too near the edge and then away, and he held her closer.

But now she was pulling away, and he was drawing her in, tighter. She worked out of his arms, but he was stronger and grappled her back. It was more than an embrace now, and I heard her say, "No."

She went rigid as she had when she'd stepped back from the snake. He had her by the wrist, and his words must have been low and urgent. She lunged forward to throw him off-balance. He nearly went into the pool, but he danced a moment alone to catch himself. She turned in a furl of her skirt and ran the long way around the pool and up the steps into the house.

When I turned back to my room, the hairbrush was still in my hand. I remembered the safe place where I'd put my return ticket, and I pulled out my luggage to pack for home.

CHAPTER 8

BROOKE TWISTED IN MY DAD'S GRASP AND STRUG-gled away from him through all my dreams. I awoke burned to an ash with anger. I was up before the rest, and I'd need some help.

Dressed to go, to leave and never come back, I started through the house. It was cool at this hour, cooler than I was. I surprised a lizard on a wall. It froze and pretended to be a crack in the plaster until I passed. Somewhere in the maze I found Martin, carrying Lucius Pirie's breakfast tray. I was probably chalk-white despite my tan, but the mask of his face never changed when I said, "I need to make a phone call." He might not even speak English, but he had know-ing eyes.

"The only telephone is in Mr. Pirie's quarters." His English was perfect. "Perhaps he will let you use it if you follow me." He was older than I'd noticed, far from being a boy. His white hospital shoes made a little sound along the tile of the halls. He turned through a door and on the other side was a sudden spiral of stairs. He stopped at the top, keeping me back. "The young lady to see you," he said above me. Then he stepped aside, the tray in one hand, to let me go first.

The room at the top of the house was large and high-ceilinged. I couldn't make much sense of it. Lights that had burned through the night were still on. The bed was monumental, stacked all around with books. There were paintings everywhere, framed and unframed, hanging, leaning. A massage table stood in the middle of the room and in the corner was a cylinder of oxygen. A scent of medicine hung in the air.

At the far end, the room thrust out onto a deck over the bay, ranked with potted flowers and overgrown with bougainvillea. Lucius Pirie sat in an old wicker-sided wheelchair. Here in his quarters he could conserve his strength, and I saw what it cost him to come downstairs for his guests. He was at the edge of outdoors, half in the light, casting a shadow the length of the room. In a vast pair of striped pajamas, he was turning slowly my way. "Ah, that young lady."

One hand gestured in the way he communicated with Blanca, and so I had to move toward him. I was pretty sure he didn't welcome company in his quarters. Martin moved past me, to fit the tray on a table over Lucius Pirie's knees.

"Breakfast," he said, "and then to bed. What can we do for you this morning?"

"I'd like to use the telephone . . . please."

He exchanged a glance with Martin, who was unfolding the napkin for him. There was a rose on the breakfast tray.

With Martin's help, I called my mother. I heard the phone ringing familiarly at home, and her voice rising from sleep. I hadn't heard her voice in ages. "Jessie?" she said.

"Mom. I'd like to come home."

And Mom said, "Here I am."

Martin called the airline for me, in Spanish. I was lucky because this was New Year's Eve day, and the planes weren't full.

Still I could have left, waving good-bye to mysterious, awesome Lucius Pirie across the room. But Martin guided me back to him. Quietly he said, "You may sit with Mr. Pirie while he has his breakfast. I will drive you to the airport in good time."

I wasn't asked why I wanted to leave so soon and suddenly. There was an extra cup of tea from somewhere, and Lucius Pirie shared his breakfast toast with me. I hadn't noticed before, but he ate with precision. His fingers were big wrinkled sausages, but he buttered the toast as if he were applying brush strokes. Martin had slid me into a chair.

"You are named for your mother, I believe?" Lucius Pirie said, glancing up.

"My grandmother. Grandmother Ferris."

"Yes, of course," he said, waving toast. "The generations get by me. I think I've never had the pleasure of meeting your mother. You'll be going back to her today. Chicago." He felt a chill and trembled, sensing the wind off Lake Michigan.

I was hungry again for the first time in days.

"Difficult for young people today, racketing back and forth between mothers and fathers," he said. "The changes in climate alone . . ."

He may have dozed. The wheeze might have been a snore. But he stirred. "Young people," he said. "That young man, Tony, who hangs on my every word. And Brooke—lovely—Margo's niece. You have enjoyed their company?"

I nodded. They'd been nicer to me than they'd needed to be. Right from the start, when they met me at the airport because Dad wouldn't have gotten around to that. Tony had given me my first kiss. And I'd wanted to be Brooke, until last night. Lucius Pirie studied me. There was pink all the way around his eyes.

"You're not much like your father, poor Scotty. I suppose he has become rather like a son to me over these past months since he turned up, out of the blue as it were. The sort of son who's never at home. Are you like your mother?"

"I don't know yet."

"A good answer, isn't it, Martin?" Because Martin was just a step away, on duty. But Lucius Pirie's eyes remained on my face. "I never painted very young people," he remarked. "They aren't quite there yet, if you see what I mean."

Somehow I seemed to.

"You'll never be pretty. Be glad of that. You have a chance at something better. I wish I were to be here when you're a grown woman. I haven't held a brush in years, but I shall be sorry not to see you."

Suddenly I was sorry, too, to know him just as I was going, as he was going. It was all upside-down, like everything else, and he'd said something wonderful about me, for me to keep. I'd have wanted to stay here if it could be the two of us.

"I suppose my paintings are my true children." He gestured back at the pictures around the room. "Like a father, I've sometimes thought they cost me too much, but they are like children, something of me to leave behind. And this house.

"This house and I have become one another. We have settled in among these quaking rocks. Even the occasional earth tremor only wedges us in more firmly." He looked up. "Martin, wheel me out onto the deck. Jessica won't have seen the view from here, and I save the best one for myself."

I could have wheeled him, but Martin had whisked away the breakfast table and was already there behind the chair. I followed them out onto the deck, and these last glimpses were growing precious. The bay was more like a horseshoe from here, and the morning sun hadn't yet robbed it of any color. The rocky arms that made the bay reached out into the sea.

"The local people have always called those two long peninsulas *Amor y Muerte,* love and death. I believe that farther point of land is *love* and this nearer one *death.* I can't think why. Some legend. Some pre-Aztec maiden with an unpronounceable name may have leapt from one high rock to save her honor. Or some brave young warrior, crossed in love, may have flung himself from the other. Most legends come to that. But it was a name to build into my house. I raised it out of love for this place and for the beauty of its people. Here I shall fetch up my last breath."

He waved to Martin to take him back inside. His skin was like a centuries-old turtle, and I'd have kissed him good-bye, but it wasn't yet time for me to go.

"Your grandmother was a beauty, as you know." I stood by his chair in case he wanted to take my hand. "Beautiful as a young woman. We never met later. Our paths diverged. You won't remember her, I expect. But I fancy that my brush caught her in her prime. I suppose you know her from that portrait?"

"Yes," I said. "When I was little, I thought I might see her hand move."

"Ah. I'll take that as a compliment. I hope that portrait will come to you one day, so you can remember her, and me."

"It's gone," I said, staggering under my anger. "Dad—poor Scotty—sold it to people who live over there."

I pointed across the bay to the awful house where Dad and I had visited the awful people with the awful Christmas tree. The portrait of my grandmother hung in one of their rooms.

Dad had sold it to them because he wanted to live in places where it's always summer and the fishing's good. He wanted a big roll of money in his pocket and people to like him. I'd rather remember that I blurted it out, that I told on Dad without thinking. But I didn't. I'd awakened that morning ready to punish him for being who he was and not what I wanted him to be.

Martin moved up on me to protect Lucius Pirie, but it was too late. I couldn't bring the words back. I shouldn't have told. I should have let Lucius Pirie believe that the unfinished portrait of Jessica would hang in all the houses I would ever live in, a link between us. A little older, a little kinder, and I'd have lied.

His hand with the big turquoise stone tightened over the wheelchair arm. But he shook his head at Martin.

"Art collectors, are they?"

"Drug money, I expect," I said.

"Ah."

He opened his hands. "You were not wrong to tell me." But Martin wasn't so sure about that, and it showed in his eyes. He was there to stand guard against the world, and here again I was the eager enemy within the gates.

"No, Martin," Lucius Pirie said, "the shock will not kill me. It is hardly a surprise. At my age, one gets only the surprises one deserves."

The shock didn't kill him. I went back to my life, and Lucius Pirie died five winters later.

MUERTE

From the Preface to *Lucius Pirie's Mexico:*

*I was born after the turn of the century into easy cir-
cumstances in the city of Chicago. My father, Alonzo Pirie, had risen in life from a clerk in the offices of the
stockyards. Having amassed a comfortable fortune for his
time, he married Adelaide Wrightman. There were two
children of this union. My younger sister, Jessica, married
Tom Ferris of the Midstates Bank and became what was
known in her day as an ornament to Chicago society,
fulfilling our mother's hope.*

*In those years after the Great Fire, Chicago rose as a
fine, philistine city. My father built a substantial house off
the Dearborn Parkway, and there I grew up. The house*

was prey to the winds off Lake Michigan that were thought to be bracing. Stout child though I was, I felt the cold cruelly and dreamed of the warmth and color of the tropics I had never seen.

Nor had I any bent for business. My father despaired of me, but an art master at the Latin School saw promise in some of my simple sketches, still lifes, as I recall. My parents, much relieved that I showed promise of anything, would have packed me off directly to Paris, but the First World War was raging. Instead, I did some rudimentary study at the Art Institute and developed an early talent, or perhaps the knack, for portraiture.

This was the application of art that Chicago came nearest to understanding. As my mother was modestly well received in the circles of meatpackers' and merchants' wives, I did not want for commissions.

I worked from a studio fashioned out of a turret of our house, and while the world did not precisely beat a path to my door, I made an income from my work. This greatly astonished my father, who found I was self-supporting at just the time I might have been expected to drain him with my college expenses.

My plan was to find a world more vibrant than the muted grays of coal-fired Chicago. In time I made good my escape, leaving without quite finishing a portrait of my sister. I had made a pact with myself to go, on the day I had amassed three thousand dollars, to keep me until I might attain a larger fame and fortune.

In Mexico I found more than that. I have found an

Eden replete with serpents, a land of flowers and sorrow.
In it I discovered a love for the only work I know and for
the land and the home I eventually built. Here I have
been made as welcome as artists ever are, anywhere. So far
from home I've found mine in this place. If there is more
to my story, it is in the paint on the canvas that must tell
it.

L.P.

CHAPTER 9

MAYBE LUCIUS PIRIE FEARED THAT HE'D LOSE ALL his paintings, his life's work, one by one to my dad, who might sell them to pave his way in the world. The unfinished portrait of Jessica was the only painting its artist had hoped would always be in our lives and over our mantel, never sold, never in the hands of strangers.

Whatever his reasons, my great-uncle sent my father packing, perhaps on that New Year's Eve. Was Dad angry at me for getting him thrown out of that Eden? I didn't want to know. But I doubt if he was too upset. There are other Edens, and he'd know how to find them.

After Mexico, he was only the occasional postcard.

The following summer he wrote a letter to say he was thinking of getting married again. She must have been older. He said her children were grown, that she owned half a television station in Fort Worth. Though he wished I could be there for the wedding, it was to be only for the immediate family. He sent regards to my mother.

I'd gone home to her on that New Year's Eve from Mexico, scoured of baby fat by my sickness and riddled with guilt. When the cab pulled up at the canopy, Vince lunged out in his greatcoat and climbed a hill of frozen slush to welcome me back. I used the key in the front door, and my mother heard. Before she got there, I peeled off the Windbreaker so she could see my new waist. I was shades darker, and I drew in my cheeks to make my eyes even bigger.

I was early, and she wasn't looking for me yet. We met in the living room, which seemed enclosed now after where I'd been. Steam sang in the pipes, and the fireplace logs waited for evening, to be lit. My mother had on her bathrobe, and she hadn't gotten around to her hair. She could get lost in her work and never find herself all day.

I smiled, met her eyes, did a lot of new things like that.

For some reason she glanced aside to the wall where Jessica's portrait had hung. She never hung another picture there, even later when she did over the room to make it more ours and less Ferris Family.

We kept a little distance in those first moments together.

"Did I throw you in at the deep end?" she said.

"Pretty deep."

"And it *was* me," she said. "He didn't send for you."

"No. I know."

"I was afraid he wouldn't even manage to meet your plane."

"He didn't."

"You haven't come back . . . hating him?"

No. In jealousy and anger I'd lashed out at my dad, who could only be a hero when he wasn't there. You can't hate people you've betrayed unless you want to be fourteen forever.

We brought in trays for supper before the living-room fire. I was freezing, wearing two sweatshirts. But the fire had a nice crackling sound, and it was New Year's Eve, so we ate late. Down in the street the revelers tooted cardboard horns. The wind whined at the window, hoping to be invited in.

When the fire was just heaps of orange coals, Mother said, "What was she like?"

"Who?"

"Whoever." She meant Margo, and so I thought

she must know about her, but she didn't. "Your dad would have to have someone. He couldn't be alone. I thought we could make a marriage out of that. I was very young at the time."

"She was okay."

Mom smiled at that. "She was good-looking. She had a great figure, and charm, and money of her own. And she had her own agenda."

Margo seemed to materialize right there before us. "How did you know that?"

She pointed up to the pale place above the mantel. "He had a mother rather like that."

"The original Jessica."

"You were named for her over my objections."

"Well, she was beautiful."

"I believe she was at one time," Mom said. "When I knew her, she was an old battle-ax. She'd been married years and years before Scott was born, and so he was this miracle son to her, and she spoiled him and ruined him. She wasn't too happy to see me on her turf. I never got him away from her. This is the old Ferris apartment, you know."

That may have been the moment she decided to redecorate.

"Will we lose it—in the divorce?"

"This apartment? Oh, no. I made the mortgage payments on it for years. You can't imagine how fast your dad went through his family's money. I own this place outright now. It's in my name."

"Will there be alimony?" I said, innocent still.

"If there is," Mom said, "I won't pay it."

It was midnight, and bells rang out in the frosty night. Mom and I raised a couple of glasses of cherry ginger ale and toasted the new year. "And to your dad," she said, clinking rims, "whatever he's up to tonight."

"You loved him though," I said.

"Who wouldn't? He was a young girl's dream. Wasn't he?"

"Do you miss him?" I asked, missing him.

"Oh, Jess, I missed him when he was here."

From somewhere you could hear "Auld Lang Syne" drifting in.

"Dad says you'll probably marry again."

"Men always say that," Mom said, "on their way out the door. It eases their consciences. Maybe women say it on the way out the door too. I don't know. I haven't left anybody."

Over the rim of her glass she gave me a long look. "I won't leave you," she said. "I can only be one parent, and so there'll be some roles I can't play. And there'll be times when I'll be all over you when you want me off your case and out of your way. But I won't leave you."

The dying fire made little remarks. I was happy to be home and a little homesick for Mexico. Maybe it was the warmth of the fire on my face.

"You're all different," Mom said. "Very svelte."

"I ought to be. I threw up everything but my socks for two days and nights."

Mom slapped a sofa pillow. "I knew it. Didn't I say so? I was afraid you'd get sick, and I couldn't see Scotty sitting by your bedside."

I didn't tell her it was Margo who'd sat there. I didn't tell everything I knew, and so there was hope for me yet. The orange ashes settled around the andirons and threw out one last coal.

"You understand why I sent you down there, don't you?"

I nodded. It was so I could sit before this fire and welcome the new year with my mother. I could stop living in my room now, with only the bulletin board for company. But it had been a long trip from the bedroom to the living room.

Then I was back at school. Rhonda wasn't very impressed with my tan. As a matter of fact, that was her last year at our school. She ruled us to the end, but she didn't come back that next fall. We heard her father had become the fall guy in something called a leveraged buyout. The rumor was that they'd lost everything and had to start over in a western suburb. It was said that Rhonda was in a public school. We followers found she was a habit we could break, and after Rhonda we got to choose our own friends.

That September my class moved on to the upper school. How long we'd waited to get here, and now we'd made it onto the bottom rung. But it was still a girls' school, and so talking about guys endlessly and in the abstract was a sort of artform, our main extracurricular activity. If Rhonda had still been with us, she'd have had a boyfriend—at a distant school in another city. Some bronzed god she'd met on the beach at St. Lucia. She'd have told us all about him. We wouldn't have believed, but we'd have listened. I never told anybody about Tony. He'd begun to fade, and besides, he'd have sounded like a figment of my imagination. In fact, he was becoming one.

Remembering Brooke, I left my hair long, below the shoulders. It wasn't as dark as hers, and the effect wasn't the same. But I recalled her way of running a hand quickly through it, and borrowed that.

And of course I wrote to her—reams. It got me through homework: Latin verbs and the monotonous mysteries of geometry. There came that magic moment in the evening when I could sweep the desk clean and arrange the blank sheet of paper formally before me and write *Dear Brooke* in graceful letters that grew more confident and Brooke-like every time.

Dear Brooke, I'd write, *today at school . . .* I told her about the senior girls who reminded me of her; of Monica, who was met after school every day down at the corner by the mysterious guy in black leather on a motorcycle; of the way Monica's hair flipped as she fitted on the hard helmet and climbed on behind; of how they roared away while we watched through the fence.

Dear Brooke, I'd write, about Mr. Ettinger, the new social studies student teacher. *He has eyes the color of the bay at Acapulco, and he wears Banana Republic tan shirts with wool ties pulled loose, and construction boots. A class full of girls makes him blush. We watch a kind of sunset color rising up his neck to take over his face. I'm circulating a petition to maintain the ecological balance of Lake Michigan because he wants us to get involved. . . .*

I didn't make a lot of friends, but when I did, I told Brooke. I wrote to her about Cara who wasn't as overbearing as Rhonda or too-beautiful-to-be, like Brooke. Cara's parents were divorced too. It wasn't exactly a rare occurrence. "They fought for years," Cara said. "They threw compact discs at each other. It went on and on."

"So you were prepared when they split up," I said.

And Cara answered, "Nobody's prepared."

I put things like that in my letters, to relive and look at on the page. *Dear Brooke,* I'd write, and one night Mother burst in on me. I never had completely cured her of walking right into my room like she owned the place, which of course she did.

"Who are you writing to?"

"Nobody," I said, and it was true. I never sent any of the letters. I didn't have Brooke's address, and now she'd be at Middlebury. In the counselor's office at school I'd leafed through the Middlebury College catalogue, imagining her walking across the snowy campus against a backdrop of those severe New England buildings and cold evergreen hills. I couldn't really picture Brooke there, muffled in L. L. Bean. I could only see her sunlit by the lush colors of Mexico or by the subtle candlelight of evenings that hadn't begun to cool. After a while I couldn't really imagine her at all. I had stopped wanting to be someone else.

"I have this imaginary pen pal," I said, answering Mom.

"Someone to talk to who understands everything and never interrupts?"

"Like that."

"Be careful, my girl," she said. "You could end up a writer. It could be in your genes, just waiting to attack."

My mother is a writer. I'd always known. She

didn't do clerical work for other people. But when Dad left, I'd wanted her to be this gray nothing who sat in the room behind the kitchen, doing dumb, mindless work. I wanted to take everything away from her.

Now I began to leave the door of my room halfway open in case she wanted to drop in. Still, there were times when that rambling apartment wasn't big enough for the two of us. Moody times like the approach of my fifteenth summer. I wasn't the camp-counselor type. My zeal to preserve the planet had departed with Mr. Ettinger, and I was too young for a summer job. Mom gazed into corners where nobody was, trying to decide something.

"How would you like a job this summer with me?" she said in her least-definite voice. If it had anything to do with her career, she was breaking her old rule about keeping the world away from that little room behind the kitchen.

"Me? What could I do?"

She was still thinking about withdrawing the offer. But she was also going to have me on her hands all summer.

"The publisher in New York answers most of the mail from my readers," she said. "But they're short-handed in the summer, and I said I'd take on some of the answering myself."

"People write to you?" I said. "Readers?"

Mom seemed to be having an attack of modesty, or something. She was also opening a door to herself and letting me in, and it wasn't easy for her. "Yes, they write to me. You could answer some of them."

"My typing's pretty bad."

"I thought it might be more personal to answer in longhand, just a note, something friendly."

That was my summer. Mom and I wedged into her little hideaway with an air-conditioner whining in the only window. I set up office in the corner, and I got serious about the job, even wore a green eyeshade. Mom was used to working alone, very programmed. She sat with all her research around her, in a special pair of house shoes, very ratty. She had this special bottle of fern-scented hand cream to put on before she got started. She went through all these rituals, and in the midst of her writing she'd sometimes call the word processor a name I never heard her use otherwise.

I remember that first June day and how awed I was at the size of the first sack of mail. I used a kitchen knife to open the envelopes, all shapes and colors of envelopes and paper. There are people with some really strange taste in stationery. Then I began to read. It was interesting right from the start, reading other people's mail. And surprising.

"Mom, you write novels."

She was putting on her hand cream and hadn't started working yet. "I know."

"Mom, you are—"

"I know that too," she said. "But I like not being known. I like the privacy of it and the freedom and because it works this way."

"You mean nobody knows who you are, as a writer?"

"My friends know. Marge Brennan knows. And Vince."

"Vince?"

"He brings up the mail."

"Why didn't I know?"

"You never asked."

And I hadn't. When I was a child, she was mommy. When Dad left, she was the enemy. And now—now we were these two human beings with a load of work to do in this little room. I was astounded at how often I seemed to meet my mother for the first time.

I reached for a fresh envelope and began addressing my first reply.

That was my fifteenth summer. In my junior year, Dad came back.

CHAPTER 10

JUNIOR YEAR, SOMEHOW, WASN'T AS NEAR BEING seniors as we'd hoped. We had to do junior-year projects, but that wasn't until the spring. One of the things I remember best about that whole year happened on one ordinary night in the fall.

Four or five of us, including Cara, were going out to a movie. It was like a lot of other nights, but I even remember being in my room, getting ready. I'd taken down Dad's pictures by then. My bulletin board had turned to other topics. At the movie we passed popcorn and comments, and grabbed each other's arms whenever Jeremy Irons came on the screen.

There wasn't any warning. I was just on my feet, pushing past people to get to the end of the row and out of there. Cara followed me, running up the aisle because I was running.

In the lobby she said, "Jess, are you sick?"

I wasn't, though I couldn't catch my breath. "There's something wrong at home," I said. Somehow I was sure of it. "I've got to get home."

"I'll come with you," Cara said, but I wouldn't let her. I had this picture strong in my mind. I knew what I was going to find when I got home, and I didn't want anyone else to know. I was running down streets, and the city blurred past me. The faster I ran, the clearer the picture in my mind.

Then I was darting into the lobby, past the night doorman. I was in the elevator, fumbling for the door key. In the apartment, almost blind now, I didn't know where to turn. There was a light in the living room, but I couldn't even see Mom until she came out of the wing chair where she'd been reading. "What on earth?" she said.

I was trembling, cold and scared, but she was here, coming toward me. "What is it?" She held me in her arms. "What?"

When she'd settled me down, I told her the crazy idea that had come over me for no reason at the movies. I was certain that Mom had left. That she'd waited for me to go out, and then she'd packed all her things, and maybe some extra things, and she'd left, gone away, for good. And now there was nobody.

Even when I was home and it had all been a weird vision, I was still shaking.

"An aftershock," she said. "Just telling you once a long time ago that I wasn't going to leave you, too, wasn't enough."

"I could be losing my mind."

"Though you probably aren't," she said. "When families break up—when big, threatening changes happen, you still have to deal with the effects years afterwards. You can't cope with it all at once. I know."

"You do? How?"

"There are times when I feel sorry for myself and so bitter I can taste it. There are times when I feel like such a failure."

I couldn't believe it.

"Mom, you're a big success."

She only smiled, and my fears faded in stages. We actually had a pretty nice evening together then. "You do know, don't you," she said at the end of it, "that one of these days you'll be the one packing up and moving out."

That May we had to present our junior projects to the entire upper school. At first I didn't know what to do for mine. Anything scientific was out of the question, and fortunately I'd never written poetry. Then I thought of something. Actually Mrs. Dowling, the upper school librarian who seemed to know everything, thought of it because it was so right I hadn't thought of it myself. I started reading up and prepared a sort of script.

My mother needed a lot of convincing about turning up at school as my project, let alone making a speech. I'd heard her on the phone turning down spots on TV shows, national network TV shows. I had to work on her for over a month. She said that what she wrote wasn't intellectual enough for a school setting. It was a junior project just getting her organized, and she was full of excuses.

Finally, I said, "I know, Mother. The cat ate your gym suit, but you're going anyway." That brought up the whole problem of what she was going to wear. She went down to Field's and came back with four new outfits from the skin out and still couldn't decide.

"Look here," she said, glued to the mirror and pointing at her temple. "Look at all this gray hair. Where'd it come from? Should I have a rinse put on it, or would that look cheap? Which would embarrass you less?"

"Mom, please, you're going to look great."

"Am I?" she said, almost like a kid.

"You're going to look great," I said, softer.

She did, though when I was leading her into school, she said she'd rather pay another eleven years' tuition than go through this. Word got out, and people's mothers wanted to meet her. Her friends turned out. Mrs. Brennan came down from Evanston, though Mom warned her not to sit in the front row. At the last minute I had some stage fright myself, but when we were both up there and people clapped, I knew it was going to be all right.

I just talked a little about Mom and her work. By then I'd read it all. I told them how many languages she'd been translated into and held up some copies of her books. I held up *Love's Incandescence,* which I'd taken to Mexico with me all those years ago, and then I introduced my mother by her pen name, Angela Chatsworth.

Long ago I'd disappeared into *Love's Incandescence* because it would take me far away from my mother, not to mention the emptiness my father left behind. I wouldn't have read the first line of that book if I'd known who'd written it.

The afternoon was beautiful, and after the school program we were both too revved up to go straight home. Mom said she might make it as much as a mile in the shoes she was wearing, and so we headed down Michigan Avenue. We admired the jonquils coming out around the Water Tower, and we had tea up in the lobby of the Four Seasons and admired each other.

When we got home, the new afternoon doorman said there'd been a caller when we were out, a man to see Mom. On the way up in the elevator, I asked her if she was finally getting around to dating. She always said she was going to get around to that, even though she didn't meet a lot of eligible men back in her writing room.

But we hadn't been home long before the doorbell rang. A version of Dad stood there, not so much older, but a little shorter. Or was I taller? It isn't that I didn't know him. I suppose it didn't seem real.

I'd changed more than he had. In the first instant he didn't recognize me, but then he said my name. That made me thirteen again, and it was the day he'd come back to take away the unfinished portrait of Jessica, and the Ferris family silver. He wasn't wearing a flight jacket now. He wore a tweed coat and a sky-blue preppie shirt, another college-boy look that struck me as too young for him.

I felt like shutting the door in his face. It would erase my guilt and maybe his and keep the past where it belonged. He stepped nearer, brushing my cheek with a kiss. He hadn't gone back to a mustache.

In the living room, he looked around. After all, this was the home where he'd grown up, maybe the only

home he'd ever had. Mother had lightened the room
with Laura Ashley at the windows and Colefax &
Fowler on the old Ferris wingchair. But even when
she'd had the walls covered in pale gray linen, she'd
left that space above the mantel blank.

He stood there now in front of the fireplace. Mom
came in and found him there, and me hovering.

"Scott?" she said, almost unsure.

He wheeled around to see her. I saw her through
his eyes. She hadn't changed out of her new clothes,
and I was glad. All she lacked were the ancestral earrings, which neither one of us had much occasion to
wear. She was good-looking. She had a great figure,
and charm, and money of her own. And she had her
own agenda.

They were both wonderful-looking people meeting
again after years, like in a miniseries. He put out both
hands. She put out one.

He divided between us, but mostly his eyes were
on her. He wasn't ready for me. I looked too nearly
grown, and that would make him older. Did he realize how much time had passed?

I hadn't written to him. His postcards never in-
cluded a return address. Had he married the Fort
Worth woman with the immediate family and the television station? He'd never mentioned her again, and
he wore no wedding ring, but then he wouldn't.

He was in Chicago overnight on business. He said he was in sales now, but he didn't say what he was selling. He wanted to take us out to dinner, and I pictured the three of us in some well-lighted restaurant. We looked good. It wouldn't be sad or might-have-been. I wouldn't have minded.

But Mom said, "I don't think so, Scott. You didn't give us any forewarning, and I have a load of work to get through. Why don't you spend the evening with Jessica?" Briefly, the ghost of Margo flitted through the room.

Actually, Mom hadn't meant to work this evening. We'd both planned to go back to school for a reception, a wrap-up party for the junior class after our projects. It was the kind of school that still has receptions with a punch bowl on a lace tablecloth in the library. Mom looked at me and sent a silent message. That's how I happened to take my dad to a school function, his first.

She eased us efficiently out of the apartment when it was time to go. We were on our way before he quite knew. "It was good to see you again, Scott," my mother said at the door. "It really was."

I'd been having bouts of stage fright all day. Now I had another. I didn't want to be alone with Dad. I didn't want him to accuse me of anything, and I'd forgotten now what I'd wanted to accuse him of. Seeing him made me younger, and tonight I needed to be older.

In the elevator we stood apart and looked for topics. He lingered in the elegant old lobby with the coffered ceiling and the brass chandelier. This place was his boyhood.

Then we were walking up the school steps. He'd taken my hand in his square grip and given it a squeeze. And it was going to be all right. He was Dad again for those moments, taller. It was like living someone else's life. I knew when we walked into the party that he'd be the best-looking man in the room.

I didn't even have to introduce him around. People came up to him. I didn't have to explain this sudden Dad. Half the school were without dads or with part-time dads or with dads who come and go, though it had taken me a long time to realize that.

He said all the right things to my teachers. Mrs. Dowling took both his hands in hers and gazed raptly up. The minute Cara met him, he drove Jeremy Irons right out of her mind. I watched him to see if he was taking credit for me when he had no right to. But he didn't. When I stood a little apart from him, he let me. He swam through the party with easy strokes, and people liked him.

He took me out for dinner to a little place he remembered. He was looking for The Acorn on Oak where he said he and Mom used to go, but it was closed now. "Usually I don't look back," he said. "It's best not to, so tonight's special."

We went someplace else, a dim room not too crowded. I was torn between wanting to leave and wanting this to last. I knew there'd be things I'd wish later that I'd said. The candle on the table between us was in a tacky red bowl with plastic fishnet, but candlelight reminded me of a place I hadn't meant to mention.

"Mexico," I said. "Remember?"

I didn't ask him about Lucius Pirie. I knew Dad had never gone back, couldn't go back. And now I knew he wasn't going to blame me for betraying him about the picture he'd sold or about Margo or about anything.

"Mexico," he said. "We had a great time, didn't we?"

He didn't tell me about the business he had in Chicago. He only talked about places he'd been, important people he'd met. When it was time to go, he said, "How well your mother looks. Better than ever."

I thought then how funny fate was to bring him back on this particular day. Any other time, and he'd have found Mom in her bathrobe and her writer's shoes with her hair on end. Today he found her pulled together and glossy, like all the women he admired most. I smiled at that, and he thought it was for him. "And what a good job she's done with you, Jess."

The candlelight created our space, as in that Mexican courtyard. But we'd filed Mexico neatly away. I thought we were going then. He'd paid the waiter. I'd folded and refolded the napkin in my lap.

"I thought your mother might have married again."

"I know."

"And how has all this been for you?" He turned his hand over to represent these past years. I only knew later what I wished I'd said. That his going away had showed me the world isn't as safe a place as I wanted it to be. But it's still a possible place.

"I'd like to come back," Dad said. He trained his eyes on me across the candlelight, and they were as hopeful and sincere as a boy's. "I'd like to come back to you both. We've lost enough time as it is."

But we hadn't. I nearly blurted it out that Mom and I hadn't, not really. I sat too still, understanding now why he was here, and what he was selling. "I'd like to be with your mother again, and I think I can get her back."

Now there was something too sure in his eyes, and I looked away because there was something sure in mine too. He couldn't get her back. He'd moved out, but she'd moved on.

I could have cried then, just for him and what he didn't see. And I had another stab of guilt, which must be my favorite emotion. Guilt because I wasn't going to be able to bring them together again. And wouldn't if I could. And it wasn't my job.

And he knew. I sat there looking down, and he knew.

Dad knows how to walk away, but we couldn't leave it at that. Out in the street in the spring night, I reached for his hand and took it in mine and held it to comfort, not cling. There was a lump in my throat. I reached around it and far back into the past, so far back it was safe.

"Dad, do you remember the Halloween I wanted to go trick-or-treating? You took me on the elevator from floor to floor. Remember pressing all those buttons because I wanted to go to every door in the building?"

"I remember," he said. "And your favorite costume was a skeleton that glowed in the dark."

I seemed to remember it was a ballerina costume with toe shoes, but that was close enough. "I loved Halloween."

"So did I," Dad said, "but what are you going to do when you're grown up?"

"What are you?" I said, and so we left it on a smile.

He went away and became a postcard again. He didn't come back for my graduation, but it was all right. By then I could love him as I love him now, at a distance, without expectations. And hardly a trace of guilt.

Chapter 11

After all those years in a girls' school, I wanted a thoroughly coed college. It turned out to be picture-perfect, in a little courthouse town in Iowa. There was a church spire over the chapel, and in the fall the maple trees blazed red and yellow across the campus. Because I was from Chicago, they seemed to think I should be sophisticated, and I tried to live up to the role. I wore a lot of black and refused to go through sorority rush.

But the wholesomeness of the place overtook me. In the sunny days of autumn our professors held class outdoors on the campus grounds as the brilliant leaves fell around us. Snow fell on the last day before Christmas vacation, and so the campus was a charcoal drawing, an expert one. This was always the season that reminded me of Mexico all those years ago. Warm, over-colored memories of Mexico played at the edge of my mind against the stark whiteness of a northern winter.

When I came home for vacation, my mother said I'd had a call from Tony Rhodes.

I couldn't think who that was, and then five years dissolved, and it was Tony. "He was calling from Mexico," Mother said. "He's down there to be with Lucius Pirie. I think they've always kept in touch."

I hadn't. What had I thought about Lucius Pirie? That we'd barely overlapped. I'd put him on a dim shelf at the back of my mind and hoped he'd forget the me I was.

"Tony wonders if you could come," Mother said.

"To Mexico?"

"I believe Lucius Pirie has very little time left," she said quietly, watching me. There in the steam-heated apartment with the ice on the windows, I remembered the musk of evening breeze in Mexico, how it stirred the netting around the bed. Waxy white flowers fell across a dinner table in a courtyard and distant voices echoed.

"But why me?"

"You're family," Mother said.

I hadn't even taken off my coat, and the Christmas

vacation stretched ahead. We'd planned a quiet one. Christmas dinner at the Brennans and a few days together cross-country skiing in Wisconsin.

"You can go if you want to," Mother said.

"I'd like to," I said. "Will you come with me?"

We felt on our faces the odd, off-season chill of the air-conditioning at the Acapulco airport. In a time warp, I was once again looking for a familiar face in the crowd.

Did I expect him in running shorts and barefoot with a white stroke of zinc oxide on his nose? I recognized Tony at first by his arms folded in front of him. He wore a white dress shirt with rolled up sleeves, white pants, shoes. The same shock of blond hair, but no Ray-Bans propped up on top of his head.

He was looking at us and didn't know us. He'd never met my mother and couldn't seem to believe me.

"Tony?"

"It can't be. Jessica?" I reached out for him. We were about the same height now. He was like a good-looking older brother of himself. He held me at arm's length. "Aren't you supposed to be shorter, shapeless, and often on the warpath?"

My mother enjoyed that. His rental car was nothing like his old Day-Glo low-rider, but he'd parked it at

random, with one wheel up on the curb. The highway
was unchanged, crumbly, with all the little thatched-
roof stands along the roadside. A runaway pig was
loose, dodging traffic in all the lanes. We hit bottom
when we turned onto the dirt road to the sea. There
again were the wandering fences and the strange veg-
etation that writhed underground for water.

Now at the top of the lane above the sagging arbors I saw the jumble of the house. And beyond the
rocks, a wedge of the turquoise Pacific. At the top of
the steps the tall front doors stood open.

We lingered outside with our luggage around us.
We hadn't brought much. Most of what I had was in
my old Poco-Loco beach bag, faded now. Mother had
never been to Mexico, and the full impact of it struck
her, and the colors cut at her eyes. For me, it was
something else. "Like coming home," I said to Tony.

He was older now and had crossed that invisible
border into the country of adults that was still mostly
mysterious to me. Still, he draped his arm around my
shoulder in the old way. "But inside there are
changes," he said.

It was smaller, as places are when you go back. I
could almost have reached up and touched the
painted beams. I'd remembered this place as a maze,
but it seemed simple now, and the rooms were where
I expected them to be.

At the steps down into the long living room with the sea beyond, Mother stopped stock-still. Lucius Pirie's paintings still hung here, ranking the room, glowing. They were more dramatic now that the furniture was gone. The fine tiled floor was cracked across.

"This is incredible," Mother said. "All his work together, and in this setting. What will happen to them?"

"He's made the arrangements," Tony said, "and I've helped him as much as I could. Most will go to public collections, several in Mexico and Latin America, the Art Institute in Chicago, the Modern in New York, the Tate."

He'd told me his paintings were his children, and now he was finding them homes. Mother wanted to be nearer them. They were enough to make you forget why we'd come. She and Tony made a slow circuit around the room. The paintings seemed to join them as friends. I noticed how Tony's boyishness had deepened into ease.

Without the furniture the room they circled was like a museum now. Even the sound of their footsteps echoed as in a public place. But this house couldn't last as a museum to the work of Lucius Pirie. Already nature was reclaiming it. The cracks would widen in the walls, and the rocks would thrust up through the floors because there is always change in everything, in everybody.

I saw something else in the room. Very faintly a Christmas party was going on, with little boys and girls in their stiffened clothes making their way up to the vast old man presiding from his throne in a broad Panama hat.

Tony and my mother and I were the last guests that house received. We weren't allowed to see our host on the first night. His faithful Martin was still with him, still guarding the door to the heart of the house. It was Martin who decided now, and we were willing to wait.

It was a house preparing for death, and we drifted through it that first evening, haunting it ourselves. I saw Mother imbibing its atmosphere the way writers do. Awed by it, respectful of its sorrow and yet searching already for the words to express it. Most rooms stood empty. The best of the furniture had already gone to a museum in Mexico City. The last crates stood waiting.

I showed my mother the view from the room that had been mine. The bed had been taken down, and the bedposts lay like a cord of firewood along a wall. The dusty votive light with the burned-away candle still stood in the niche.

The three of us dined that night in the candlelit

courtyard. There was only one woman left, to do the cooking. Not Blanca. She and Baltazar and all the others had received their legacies from Lucius Pirie and had gone back to their villages. He'd made all these arrangements, and Tony had helped him. Tony had come down here to be with Lucius Pirie every year of the last five. Even when he'd graduated from college and decided he wasn't an art historian, Tony came back.

We sat at the same long table, Mother at the head where our host had sat and I beside her and Tony opposite. There was only one candle, and the far end of the table stretched into enough darkness for ghosts to gather. We sat in the underwater light, tired, our conversation unreal, my mind slipping back. The food wasn't what it had been, and the woman served us with her face closed.

Tony was still in the *caseta,* and he organized a bedroom in the main house for Mother and me, salvaging the beds for it. She was tired and went to bed early. Tony and I walked down as far as the terrace with the house dark and blank-eyed behind us. No moon, but the ocean glowed.

"How do you feel about being back?" he asked me.

"Glad," I said. "Sad. When I was here before, I didn't understand anything, and I wouldn't want to leave it at that. I shouldn't have worried so much about the others—Brooke, Margo, even Dad. I ought to have sat at Lucius Pirie's feet the way you did, Tony, and learned from him and . . . forged a link. I should have—"

"Been older than you were?"

"Yes. And even now. I'm still my own unfinished portrait."

Shaking back my hair, I ran a hand quickly through it. The gesture was so much my memory of Brooke and nothing of my own that Tony grinned. One of his old grins you could see in the dark. "I thought you were in love with her," I said. "I fantasized about that."

"So did I," Tony said. "And I was nineteen, and so I had to be a little bit in love with every beautiful girl I met. I had my image to consider. But no, I couldn't have been in love with Brooke. She didn't need me. She didn't need anybody. She was like Margo. By now I expect she is Margo."

"Yes, I've thought that too," I said.

"And now you must be the age Brooke was then."

"Just about."

The memory of Brooke turned from us both and walked away in that graceful, coltish way she had. Tony and I stood looking out over the perfumed night, his arm around my shoulder, old friends now.

The next morning Mother and I had breakfast down on that terrace. It was already sun-dazzled, but so early that the bay was a painting of itself. The pool was empty and baking in the sun. This was the place where I'd first seen Margo sitting with her arm along the railing, looking out to the sunset. Lucius Pirie had been descending those steps carefully, one at a time with Martin by his side.

Tony was descending them now, to say that Uncle Lucius would see us.

"You go," Mother said. "I'll stay here. I'm a stranger, and it might worry him."

Tony put out his hand and I took it and we went. He led the way up the spiral stairs to the most private place in the house. I hoped it wouldn't be terrible. There was a faint scent of medicine.

The room was starker now. The shelves were empty, and things were standing around. Lucius Pirie was particular about his plans, and he'd overseen the packing up himself as if death were a journey.

He was there on the enormous bed, and my heart was in my throat. The bed linens were snowy, too fresh and unwrinkled for him to have spent the night on. Someone much smaller was where I expected him to be. He'd shrunk to this. His head was a small pol-ished dome almost lost in the big pillow he was propped against. With great effort he was sitting almost upright to see us. And beside him Martin, still in immaculate white. He nodded to acknowledge me, and it was a warning not to stay long.

Tony led me around the bed where Uncle Lucius could see us both. He wore a spotless nightshirt like a Mexican child's, with a drawstring at the throat. When I was near enough, he put out his hand. The huge turquoise ring hung loose.

I took his hand in both of mine. It wasn't quite human now, and the turquoise stone had already gone cold. But I wanted to hold him back. I didn't want him to go yet. Did he really know who I was? It shouldn't have mattered, but it did.

"My dear Jessica. It's been too long," he said in a high, hollow voice.

Still, he might think I was that other Jessica from longer ago. His sister.

"Do you know me, Uncle Lucius?"

His gaze was watery, but keener than I'd noticed. "Of course I know you, child. I'm dying. I'm not losing my mind. You're poor Scotty's girl.

"Ah, poor Scotty," he said. His hand was warmer in mine now, and I think he liked me holding it. "A bit of a bad penny, that boy. I fully expect him to turn up at my door in the next world. I shall await him with bated breath."

Beside me, Tony looked away, grinning wildly.

"You were very good to come," Uncle Lucius said. His hand stirred in mine.

"There isn't any place I'd rather be," I said. "I was glad that Tony sent for me."

"Tony?" Uncle Lucius said in mock surprise. "Tony was only carrying out my instructions. You can't think that I still make my own telephone calls at this stage. People would think they were receiving messages from the grave. I wanted you here. You are my family. You didn't think that poor Scotty wandering off the way he does keeps us from being family, did you?"

"No." Oh, no.

"And so I wanted to see you. You're nearly grown up, aren't you?"

"Nearly."

"You and I are both standing on new thresholds," he said.

Now there was hardly any distance between us.

"Have you found your eyes yet?" He leaned nearer.

I understood what he meant. "I'm beginning to," I said. "There was a snowfall on the campus the other day, and all the brights and browns of autumn were replaced by a sort of pen-and-ink drawing. I noticed how snow can create an abstract design out of something so familiar. Sometimes I see."

"Yes, so you do." His head was settled deeper in the pillow now. "I have something that might help you see, through the years ahead."

His other hand came up and gestured toward the room. There on the far side of the bed on an easel stood a painting, and why hadn't I seen it at once? It was the one I'd first seen in Tony's *caseta*. The painting Lucius Pirie had done from the terrace of this house, of the two long peninsulas reaching out to form the bay as it had been before people. It was *Amor y Muerte,* his finest work.

"It belongs to you now, Jessica. A companion for your journey. Try not to thank me for it. There's no need of that between us."

The painting and the room blurred, and Martin made a move. Uncle Lucius withdrew his hand from mine. "You must come again this evening," he said, "if . . . if you would like."

But I didn't want to wait—I didn't dare wait to ask him. "Uncle Lucius, is there life, after this one?"

I suppose it was a childish thing to ask, but he was so near that I thought he might have caught a glimpse of something ahead.

Beginning to doze, he blinked himself back. "A life after this one? Oh, yes. I see it as a vast blank canvas with an eternity of time and talent with which to fill it.''

He put up his hand again, this time for Martin, and Martin took it. He was asleep before we turned away.

We waited through the heat of the day. When it was too hot for the terrace, my mother sat in the deep windows and looked out at a distant blaze of bougain-villea across a roof, at the turning patterns the boats made down in the bay. The three of us began conversations we didn't finish, reaching out at moments just to take a hand. In the evening we were summoned back to Lucius Pirie. ''This time you come too, Mother,'' I said, and she did.

We followed Tony up the shadowy spiral one last time. The room was muted, and so was Martin's face. The painting that would come to me stood shrouded on its easel. It was almost time to light a light, but no one had. Uncle Lucius lay deep in the bed.

Tony and I were beside him now, and Mother stood back. Uncle Lucius's hands were composed on the smoothly turned-down sheet, and his eyes were closed. He opened them, perfectly aware.

He'd given me my legacy. Now he was down to details. One of his frail hands worked with the other, and he pulled off the turquoise ring. ''Tony,'' he said, and held it out to put in Tony's hand.

He smiled at me. But then he wondered. "Is there someone else here?"

I made room so Mother could stand there beside me. Uncle Lucius saw her, and a small flame lit behind his eyes. "How lovely," he said. "Have I painted you?"

He saw us together now. "But no," he said to Mother, "I see. You are who Jessica will be."

His gaze shifted away, and in his first breathless moment, his eyes fixed as if they saw only a vast blank canvas waiting to be filled.

ABOUT THE AUTHOR

Richard Peck is the author of seventeen novels for young readers. They include the eerie adventures of Blossom Culp, from Bluff City, Mid-America—the author's hometown of Decatur, Illinois, somewhat disguised. He attended Exeter University in England and holds degrees from DePauw University and Southern Illinois University, where he trained to be an English teacher. After twelve years he left the classroom when, he says, "teaching had become something weirdly like psychiatric social work, a field in which I was not trained."

To keep in touch with young readers, he visits about a hundred classrooms a year, school settings that appear in several of his award-winning novels, including *Are You in the House Alone?, Father Figure, Remembering the Good Times, Close Enough to Touch,* and *Princess Ashley.* "A writer needs to live in his readers' worlds as if he himself did not exist," Richard Peck says, and so he does plenty of field research, resulting in *Secrets of the Shopping Mall, Those Summer Girls I Never Met,* and *Unfinished Portrait of Jessica.*

He is the winner of the 1990 Author Achievement Award given by *School Library Journal* and the Young Adult Services Division of the American Library Association; the 1990 National Council of Teachers of English/ALAN Award for "outstanding contributions to young adult literature"; and the 1991 Medallion from the University of Southern Mississippi, which "honors an author who has made an outstanding contribution to the field of literature."

Richard Peck lives in New York City.